Sam Stone

FRANK BONHAM is married and has three sons. He has been a writer since the age of twenty. His books for young people include *Mystery of the Red Tide, Mystery in Little Tokyo, Durango Street, Mystery of the Fat Cat,* and *The Ghost Front*.

The two years Mr. Bonham spent in doing research for *Durango Street* led him to follow up with other stories for young people with similar backgrounds. *Mystery of the Fat Cat* was the first of these and *The Nitty Gritty* is the second.

ALVIN SMITH is a lecturer on Art Education at Queens College of the City of New York University. He has taught art in public and private schools in Kansas City, Kansas, Dayton, Ohio, and New York City. His paintings are represented in several permanent collections.

The Nitty Gritty

HOB NOB
POOL-PAR
22

The Nitty Gritty

by Frank Bonham

illustrated by Alvin Smith

E. P. Dutton & Co., Inc. New York

Also by Frank Bonham

Mystery of the Fat Cat
The Ghost Front
The Mystery of the Red Tide
Mystery in Little Tokyo
Durango Street

Published simultaneously in Canada by Clarke, Irwin & Company Limited, Toronto and Vancouver.

Library of Congress Catalog Card Number: 68-24719

First Edition

Contents

Illustrations

The Nitty Gritty

Chapter 1

Charlie and the Winos

"Buried in that cellar like a grave," Charlie's father muttered, stripping the meat from a sparerib with his teeth. "Living like a mole. Sleep days, work nights. There ain't but three light globes in that whole basement, an' ten stories of concrete over my head. Only time I see light is when one of you kids opens the curtains here when I'm trying to sleep."

"Does spending half your pay on liquor help?" asked Charlie's mother.

Charlie's father drank deeply from the can of beer by his plate, then shot her a look. "When it gets over half, woman, lemme know," he said. "I'll have a drink on it."

The Matthews family sat around the kitchen table. There were Charlie, his parents, and the two younger children, Buster and Callie. Charlie minded his own business, and kept forking in the food. Since he was not especially interested in the conversation, he let his mind slip out of gear like a car. Sometimes he would ease his eyes out of focus and go into a sort of trance, during which he had dreams so exciting and soul-satisfying that it was all he could do to return to reality. He would come out of such a dream like a person walking from a theater on a summer afternoon, blinking in the cruel sunlight.

"Been in jail, followed the crops, rode garbage trucks, and washed dishes," his father was saying. "Every place a Negro's supposed to go before he goes to his grave. But thisyer janitor job sours my blood. Everything they give me to work with is broke. A junkman wouldn't bid five dollars on the whole building. Then Mr. Akers jumps me when the elevator sticks."

Charlie's mother refilled the collards dish and brought it to the table.

"Matthews, I'm weeping salt tears," she said. "Why don't somebody ask what *I* done today?"

"What did you do today?" muttered Charlie absently. He was seventeen, short for his age but chunky, the oldest child. In his sleeveless sweat shirt, old jeans, and broken tennis shoes, he was a lumpy, compact figure as he huddled over his food.

"Since you ask, I did up six extra rooms," said his mother. "Because that no-good new girl didn't show up for work. There's some kind of a fat women's convention in town, and we got half the fat women in the world staying at the motel. If I picked up one

Charlie

candy wrapper, I picked up twenty. Club or not, those women can *eat*!"

"How come you don't join up?" asked Charlie, grinning.

"Give you a fat mouth," said his mother; then she laughed.

Charlie's father grumbled some more about the old building and his problems with it. Though Charlie had never seen it, the building sounded fascinating, especially the basement, a dark grotto full of machinery, plumbing, fuse boxes, and even a gleaming elevator tube spearing down a hole like an enormous needle driven into the thigh of the earth. In cold weather, Charlie's father sometimes let a down-and-outer sleep near the furnace.

If I operated that building, thought Charlie, *I'd run a secret flophouse down there. Fifty cents a head. Hot coffee a nickel.*

Some of those old winos were interesting. He had talked to them around the bars on Ajax Street, the main stem of Dogtown, a rundown section of the big city where he lived. One man claimed he had been a big lawyer before whiskey got him. Another said he had ten thousand dollars stashed away for when he really needed it. Ten thousand dollars! Dreaming of it, Charlie felt his eyes sliding out of focus, the gray, pencil-like bones on his plate blurring. The voices of his parents grew woolly in his ears, like those of bus passengers under the roar of the engine, voices from a dream.

Charlie was talking with a threadbare old man in the basement: *"Charlie," said the old wino, "I'd 'a' froze to death if you hadn't let me sleep by your furnace. I can't pay you nothing, but I'll tell you a secret. I was the engineer when this place was built. And there is a fortune right under our feet!"*

"A fortune!" Charlie said.

"And now Mr. Akers is talking about me painting the inside of the building," came Charlie's father's voice dimly.

"A hundred thousand dollars. Maybe more," said the old wino.

"How come?" Charlie asked.

"Well, when we built the basement, the owner told me not to tell anybody, but to build him a secret place where he could hide his money. So I built him a place in the floor, right over there at the bottom of the elevator shaft. A month after the building was finished, he died. It's dollars to doughnuts his money is still under the floor!"

Charlie saw himself probing around in the grease and muck with screw-drivers and a hammer. Beneath it all he found a metal plate! He was just raising the plate when a hand shook his arm roughly.

Charlie looked up, blinking. His father was leaning toward him. "What's the matter with you, Chahles? Didn't you hear what I said?"

Charlie landed flat-footed in the real world. "No. I—I was thinking about something else."

"I reckon you were. I said, 'Did you go to school today?' "

Charlie sighed. *Get on Charlie's back, everybody,* he thought, *there's plenty of room.* His mother worked days, his father nights. Between 7:00 P.M. and 9:30, they were both there to go after him as a team.

"Nope," he said.

"Did you work for Leonard Clark?"

"Yep."

"Let's see how much money you brought home."

Charlie dug into his jeans pocket. Coin by coin, he got up two dollars and forty-five cents. "There wasn't much action today," he said. "It got cloudy, and nobody gets his shoes shined if it looks like rain."

"How long were you at the shine parlor?"

"All day."

His mother's plump fingers gleaned the coins from the tablecloth, leaving the forty-five cents for Charlie. Buster, his twelve-year-old brother, chortled and reached for the money. He looked surprised when Charlie neatly snaked the coins away, with a grin.

Outside, Charlie heard a motorcycle popping

along. It sounded like one of those little Japanese motors, somewhere between a scooter and the big ones the kids called "hogs." Mr. Toia, his English and home-room teacher, rode a Japanese motor. Charlie turned his head as the motor slowed before the house.

Woops! he thought, suddenly remembering a note he was supposed to have given his parents. Digging into his pocket, he said hurriedly: "And I got something else at the shine stand. I forgot to give it to you."

"What's that?" asked his mother, looking at the smudged and folded piece of paper Charlie had laid before her.

"That's a note from Mr. Toia. Cowboy brought it from school."

Mrs. Matthews showed little interest in the note. "What's it say?"

"It says I'd better start showing up, or Mr. Toia'll get the attendance worker on me."

"Oh, they always says that," said his father.

"And it says he's coming by the house to talk to you tonight."

"*What*!" Roscoe Matthews' expression darkened, and he looked toward the street. "What for?"

Charlie heard the motor die; footfalls came up the walk. "About school, I guess," he said.

He watched his parents exchange stares. They were thinking that it was too late to turn out the lights and pretend they were not home, as they had had to do the last time his father was out of work and the re-po people were after the furniture. As between teachers and bill collectors, he thought, the Matthews family felt easier in their minds about collection people. They knew better what to expect.

The doorbell rang.

"Oh hell," Roscoe Matthews said. Then: "Well, go to the door," he told Charlie. "He's your teacher, not mine."

Chapter 2

Doctor Charlie

Charlie tried to decide what expression to wear, as he might have puzzled over what shirt to put on. A meek look? Sullen? Cheerful? His expression, he felt, should match the teacher's, and since he had been skipping school for two weeks, cheerfulness would probably not find its reflection on Mr. Toia's face.

On the other hand, Mr. Toia was different from any teacher Charlie had ever known. He was funny and interesting, yet there was no horseplay in his classes. Though he had not been teaching long, there was no handle on him for a smart-mouthed kid to swing him by. Somtimes when they came to class there would be a stack of newspapers on his desk, and that would be the textbook for that period. A newspaper! The kids went away arguing about the war or a hospital for Dogtown, instead of being half asleep and not caring which came first, John Adams or John Quincy Adams.

Again the doorbell rang. Playing it safe, Charlie

put on a poker face and opened the door a few inches.

A young man carrying a white motorcycle helmet in one hand and a scuffed briefcase in the other looked in. He was short, with dark, curly hair, and wore a yellow shirt with small black polka dots.

"Hello, Charlie," he said, with a wink.

"Hi."

"Are your folks home?"

"Uh-huh." Charlie blinked but made no move to open the door.

"May I come in?"

"Well, let him in, idiot!" Roscoe Matthews growled.

Charlie opened the door. Mr. Toia walked in. He nodded cheerfully to everyone. Charlie fumbled: "This is my dad, Mr. Toia. And my mom. And I guess you know Callie, at school. And that's Buster."

Everyone started to rise, but the teacher said, "No—don't get up. I'll just sit down over here. I shouldn't have come at dinnertime, but I wanted to be sure of catching you both at home."

"That's okay," Mr. Matthews said. Mr. Toia, seating himself on the sofa, gazed around the room. Charlie was afraid he was going to say something like, *Real nice place you've got here.* It was a very broken-down place, in fact, and a good part of their dinner conversation had to do with what a louse the landlord was not to fix the leaky roof or the rotten flooring.

For a few moments it was awkwardly silent.

"Like a can of beer?" Mr. Matthews said finally, without looking directly at the teacher.

"I sure would. Thanks."

Mr. Matthews gestured at Charlie, who sauntered into the kitchen to get a can of beer. While he was opening it, he heard his mother say, "We eat later than most folks. I get home after six. I guess you've already had your supper, haven't you?"

"Well, no. I had some work to do at school and I'm actually on the way home." Mr. Toia smiled, and waited.

Again it was embarrassingly quiet. *Well, ask him*! Charlie thought. But he knew the reason his mother hesitated was that she was not sure about the feeding of teachers. Did they eat soul food like collards and spareribs?

"We got plenty of what we got, if you'd care to have a bite with us," said Mrs. Matthews.

Mr. Toia accepted the can of beer Charlie handed him. "I wouldn't want to put you out, but if you really have plenty—" he said.

And he got up promptly, as though afraid there was a time limit on the offer. He found a chair and put it between Charlie and his father. Everyone began passing him things, bread, butter, ribs, and collards. Soon he was eating with gusto.

"I take it you ain't married," Mr. Matthews said.

"No, but I've got thirty-six kids, of which Charlie is one of the brightest. I don't get much written work out of him, but when I do, it's usually good work. The other teachers all say the same. Charlie's got a good mind."

"Uh-huh. Ain't that fine," Mr. Matthews mumbled, his eyes on his food.

"In fact, one reason I stopped by was to return a theme of Charlie's. He's probably forgotten it by now, it's been so long since he was at school." He winked at Charlie. "Remember it? 'My Uncle Baron, What a Guy.' I don't hand out many A-pluses, Charlie, but I had to dig down and give you one this time."

Mrs. Matthews laughed. "No! Did he really write something about his uncle?"

"He sure did. All I want to know is, is this a real man or a saint? As far as I could tell, he hasn't got a mortal fault."

"According to Charlie, he hasn't," said his mother. "That's my brother, Baron. Charlie's middle name is Baron. Baron stays a week or two with us every year."

"He sure is a comic!" Callie said. "I could sit for a week listening to him tell it about the racetracks where he works. He travels all around the country."

"And he plays a guitar, and sings," Buster put in. "He's sure a lot of fun."

Mr. Toia nodded. "That's what Charlie said in his theme: 'If goodness comes from the heart, his must be as big as a bucket!' "

Embarrassed, Charlie tucked his head down. The Matthews home jumped when Uncle Baron arrived on one of his visits. He told tall tales, roughhoused with the kids, and talked to Charlie man to man—even made a happy human being out of his father for a couple of weeks. He was a magician with tools, too, fixing doors that sagged on their hinges, glazing broken windows, putting up shelves. Then one morning he would be gone, and slowly his presence would fade from the house like a smile.

Mr. Toia, with a thoughtful frown, tapped a little rhythm on the top of his beer can with a sparerib. "Charlie shows a lot of class in all his work," he said. "I had high hopes for him at the beginning of the semester. But I'll have to flunk him unless he starts showing up more often."

Another awkward silence rolled in like a fog. Mr. Matthews poured some more beer down his throat, and suppressed a belch.

"Uh, well, I tell you, Mr. Toia," he said. "We ain't rich people, and sometimes we needs Chahles to work a day or two to help out."

"I can understand that," said the teacher. "But you see it's been *every* day lately."

No one answered him.

Again Mr. Toia tapped the beer can, thoughtfully. "If you could just find a way for Charlie to finish high school, it might be possible for him to get a scholarship to some college. With his ability, he might become a newspaperman or a playwright—something like that."

"Mr. Toia," Roscoe Matthews said, at last raising his eyes, "I can point out plenty of Negroes in Dogtown that went to college, and they're out of work as much as I am. Or they got a degree, and all they can do is work in some agency teaching kids to run a printing press or lay asphalt tile. So what's the point?"

Charlie raised his head. "Yeah, but there's lots of Negro doctors and lawyers, too. And social workers and—"

His father's eyes met his, smoky with anger. "If you think you're going to be a *doctor* or a *lawyer,* boy, there's something wrong with your brain. We done got ourselves an idiot," he said to his wife.

Buster giggled nervously. Callie sent a look of sympathy at Charlie. Mr. Toia leaned back in his chair, good-natured but firm.

"There's no question about whether Charlie *can* do it," he said. "The only question is whether he *will.* Right now is a very important time in his life."

Glancing at the alarm clock on the sink, Mr. Matthews said: "Right now is important to me, too, Mr. Toia. Excuse me, but I've got to go to work."

He left the table and walked to the closet. By the

way he yanked out his coat and slung it over his shoulder, Charlie could tell that he was angry. Charlie could have told Mr. Toia that he was wasting his breath trying to talk education to his father. The teacher got up and offered Mr. Matthews his hand as he went toward the door.

"Thanks very much for the dinner," he said. "I do want to talk to you again. Because with a little help, Charlie's going to do something in this world."

"Oh, he's gonna *do* plenty of things," said Roscoe Matthews. "He's going to do all the dirty things a black man has to do to make a living. But I don't want him going around carrying a briefcase and thinking he's going to be a doctor or a writer or some fool thing. Because that's just stupid, see?"

At the door, he glanced back at Charlie, and grinned. "Good night, Doctor," he said.

Mr. Toia said to Charlie's mother: "Arguing with Mr. Matthews is like playing handball with mashed potatoes. My best shots never came off the board. I hope you'll keep after him."

"Yes, sir," Mrs. Matthews said. She felt exactly the same as his father did, Charlie knew. Walking to the couch, the teacher grubbed through a disordered mass of papers in his briefcase. He pulled one out and handed it to Charlie.

"A-plus!" he said. "And there's more where that came from. Want to walk out with me?"

They walked outside to where he had parked his

motorcycle on the lawn. He tied the briefcase on a rack, talking as he worked with the straps.

"Level with me, Charlie," he said. "Do you really want to finish school?"

"Sure. But why fight it? My old man's got a head like a rock."

"Then you'll have to get even harder-headed than he is."

"Nobody's got a harder head than him. He holds all the records, man."

Sitting on the saddle of the motor, Mr. Toia adjusted the controls. "We can't blame him too much for feeling the way he does. He grew up when Negroes were lucky to get part-time manual labor. But now a lot of men and women his age are taking courses to get better-paying work, and making it. But it's a lot easier at your age than at his. So stay with it."

Charlie watched him ride off. *Stay with it! Man, the only way I'll ever finish school is by getting out of here*, he thought bitterly.

Chapter 3

Charlie the Healer

Slapping the theme against his leg, he started inside. "My Uncle Baron, What a Guy." *I'll talk to Uncle Baron when he comes,* he decided. *He's about due again.* Of course, Uncle Baron had had mighty little education himself. Couldn't write much more than his own name. Just the same, he was smart. He would understand that a kid with no high school diploma might as well cut off a leg. Then he could at least be sure of public assistance.

As he turned the knob to enter the house, some little wheels turned in his head. Lights flashed. a small motor whirred. He stood blinking while the machinery raced, buzzed, flashed, and finished by spelling out, in letters six feet high, the answer to his problem.

He hurried inside, walking on the balls of his feet and trying not to grin. He watched his mother carrying plates to the sink. Callie was helping her. Charlie dropped on the sofa and gave up fighting the grin that was struggling to bend his lips.

"Where do you reckon Uncle Baron is about now?" he asked.

"Some racetrack—wherever the horses are running," said his mother. "And needing to be walked and fed. What you grinning about?"

"Guess what I'm going to do."

"I *know* what you're going to do. Shine shoes tomorrow, or else tangle with your daddy."

"I'm going to work for Uncle Baron."

Both kids stared at him. Mrs. Matthews studied him to make sure he was not joking. Then she laughed. "Oh, my! My brother never hired anybody the longest day he lived. What would you do for Baron—grease his little old pickup truck?"

Charlie laid his arms along the back of the sofa, so sure he was that the old life of Charlie Matthews was ending like some dismal movie. He felt like yelling.

"He does lots of things. Carpentry and special jobs for rich people, and hauling and all. I'll get a driver's license so I can be hauling for him while he's working with the horses."

Sweet and sour mingled in his mother's face, as though she had bitten on a lemon while laughing. "You given any thought to whether my brother would want you tagging along, Charles? He's been a free soul all his born days. No wife, no kids—free as the wind."

"I'm not a kid any more," said Charlie. "I talk his language. I could send home fifty dollars a month, maybe more. I'd make that much on bets alone, with all the tips he gets. Last time he was here, he told me the jocks always know who's going to win."

Callie laughed. "He'll tell you anything if you listen long enough."

"He's about due, isn't he, old lady?" Charlie said.

"I wouldn't know. I don't set my clock by that brother of mine."

Later, in bed, Charlie tried to dope out where his uncle might be. If he knew, he could hitchhike there and lay it on the line: *How about me working for you? I'll go to school part time and work the rest of the time. When it's time to go to college, I'll have a scholarship and some money saved.*

He could hear Buster snoring softly on the bunk bed above his own. Ideas tumbled in his mind like alphabet blocks in a cement mixer. He closed his eyes and let himself float along in a reverie.

"Charlie," said Uncle Baron, "I may be late tonight. I got a lame horse to tend to."

And now he could even see him! He was about to step into his old pickup truck. Charlie himself seemed to be standing before a vague sort of motel cabin, with little southern pines in the background.

"What's the matter with him?" Charlie asked.

"That's what we don't know. His leg's been swole up for days. We've had the best vets in the country to see him, but they can't figure it out."

He let Charlie go along. There was this beautiful horse in a stable that smelled of sawdust and alfalfa-and-molasses feed, a buckskin horse with a tan hide as slick as satin. The owner was there, a young lady as pretty as the horse.

"Baron," she said, "the vet just left. He thinks I'll have to have King Midas destroyed."

When Uncle Baron tried to examine the swollen foreleg, the horse kicked at him. "Yes, it do look bad," he said. "He's in pain."

All of a sudden Charlie had one of those feelings he got sometimes. He could handle this horse! He was not afraid of it. It didn't seem to Charlie that the horse looked as sick as it should, for having such a bad leg.

He walked up and laid a hand on its neck. "Easy, boy," he said.

"Charlie! Get away from that critter!" Uncle Baron said.

But Charlie knelt down and ran his hand over the leg where it was swollen just above the hoof. The horse snorted and stamped. Charlie said, "Easy," and his fingertips kept stroking the sore leg. Under the hair he found something like a fine wire twisted so tight that it was buried in the flesh. He stood up and looked at the young lady.

"Have you got any enemies, Miss?" he asked.

"Well, yes," she said. "A man whose horse King Midas beat at Churchill Downs last year would do anything to get even."

Charlie got a pair of wire cutters. Then he cut the thing he had found—a thin strand of horsehair pulled as tight as a noose!

"What in tarnation!" Uncle Baron said. And the surprised girl took the cord from Charlie's hand.

"What is it?"

"It's a strangle cord some low-lifer put on this horse to make him go lame. It cuts off the circulation, but you can't even see it. He'll be all right now. He can run tomorrow."

The swelling went down rapidly. The horse sighed, and pawed at the sawdust.

"But how did you know?" asked the girl.

Charlie winked at his uncle. "Just lucky," he said. (No use telling her he had read about the trick in a Western story.)

When it was time to move on to another track, the young lady gave them an envelope with five hundred-dollar bills in it.

"Charlie," Uncle Baron said, "I don't know how I ever got along without you."

The fine line between dreaming and daydreaming had become so blurred that Charlie slipped across it into sleep before he got half the money spent.

Chapter 4

Hey, Big Spender!

Charlie arrived at Leonard's Shine Parlor in the cool smoky morning. Leonard opened early to get the trade of men waiting for buses into the city, Dogtown being an hour's ride from the central business district, where the money was. Slightly larger than a packing box, and with tiny living quarters in the back, the stand was wedged between a greasy-spoon café called Johnson's and a liquor store. Charlie and Leonard worked fast for nearly an hour. Then the work let up. A few early-bird students began to pass on the way to school.

"I'm going to take me a little break, now," Leonard told Charlie, when the stand emptied momentarily. He had been crippled by polio when he was a child and it hurt him to be long on his feet. "You better figure on going to school after I rest, Charlie," he added. " 'T ain't right for you to cut *every* day. I feel bad about it."

"That's okay, long as *I* feel good," Charlie said. But what he really felt was gloomy and left out, as he watched the kids walk by carrying books and lunches. He was sure things were not so tough that the Matthews family needed all the nickels and dimes he brought in. The trouble was, his father had never got over the time he was out of work for six months, and the re-po people had practically stripped the house before he found a job. Every time Charlie came home, somebody was carrying a chair or a table out the front door. It got so the moving men knew him by his first name.

"Hello, Charlie," they would say. "How's things?"

Things were bad—so bad that the Matthews family had to cook in the back yard because the gas was turned off, and they were burning candles for light. Charlie ate so much cornmeal mush and syrup that it gagged him to think about it.

Charlie sat down to do an off-feet shine, gazing mournfully down Ajax Street. The street looked as though a tornado had vacuumed all the trash from the city dump last night and dumped it all on Dogtown. He knew he would be sitting right here looking at it until he located Uncle Baron and took off. Dogtown was protected against accidental prosperity by a crescent of hills on the east, green now with autumn rains, and another wrinkle of hills on the west. The flatlands between the hills were patched with dry, flat, grimy neighborhoods where the juice of life had been sucked out of everything, the plants, the dead stamp-sized lawns, the people, by a pres-

Caesar

ence Charlie thought of as a great gray spider. It was called Poverty, and according to Charlie's father there was no use struggling to escape its web, because it would only wear you out so that you died sooner.

Mr. Toia, however, claimed that education made the handiest pair of tin snips you ever saw to cut your way out.

Charlie was beginning to dream of camping with Uncle Baron beside a trout stream when he heard someone say, "Morning, mahn."

Charlie blinked, and gazed at a boy standing before the shine stand. He thought he must still be dreaming, because this boy was too tall to be real. He was so tall you could have strung wires from his shoulders and nailed posters to him.

"Hi," Charlie said.

"Is Mr. Clark here?"

"Who? Oh. Yes, but he's resting." Charlie had never heard Leonard called "Mr. Clark" before. "You want a shine?"

The boy smiled, and shook his head. He was West Indian, judging by his speech.

"No, I want to work here. I talked to Mr. Clark last night about working here on Saturdays. He said maybe I could hang around, and when you and he were both busy I could take anybody else that came in. I thought maybe he'd made up his mind."

Charlie went on guard. He thought of telling him

to get lost, that there was not enough work for two boys here. But he knew Leonard would see to it that he was treated right. Also, this boy looked like one who would understand such a situation and not try to muscle anyone else out.

"He didn't say anything about it," Charlie said. "Not to me. You won't get rich here, but you might make a couple of bucks if you're lucky. You're new around here, aren't you?"

"Yes. I go to Memorial High."

"Me too," Charlie said. "What grade?"

"Eleventh."

"Got Mr. Toia for English?"

"Sure have. Nice fella. My name's Caesar Étienne," the boy added. He said it like *Eighty-yen*.

"Charlie Matthews."

They shook hands.

"Well, will you tell Mr. Clark I'm still interested?" Caesar said.

"You bet," Charlie said.

"Thanks."

The boy shifted some books under his arm. But before he could leave, four other boys came along and stood before the stand, blocking his way. They were all Memorial High kids, and Charlie said, hello; but he did not like the grin on the face of one of them, a boy they called Cowboy. Cowboy had himself confused with a television comic or someone. He looked just as ridiculous as some, but the difference was that Cowboy's jokes had little tearing barbs that drew blood.

"Shine 'em up," Cowboy said. "You getting a shine, Caesar?"

"No, mahn. I'm hoping to work here."

"Well, you hang in with my friend Charlie. Charlie's a real solid career shine man. He'll teach you all the tricks."

Charlie gave Cowboy a level stare that warned, *That's once. . . .* He had never fought with Cowboy, but he figured he could probably take him. Cowboy was a couple of inches taller, but without the solid pack of Charlie's muscles. He had a big mouth that opened like a wound when he grinned. He wore a cowboy hat pinned up in front, a yellow collarless shirt, and black levis.

"Well, I'll see you Saturday," Caesar said to Charlie.

But as he tried to pass, Cowboy moved into his path, still grinning at Charlie. The other boys were smiling too, primed for whatever joke Cowboy had promised them. "Did Toia show up last night?" asked Cowboy.

"Yeah. Why?"

"What happened?"

"Nothing happened, man. Charlie can handle any teacher you point out."

"What'd he want?"

"You read the note, didn't you? You brought it.

No, that's right—they haven't been able to teach you cursive yet, have they?"

The other boys chuckled. They had settled down to pure enjoyment of the contest. It was almost as good as a fist fight, and they knew that if things went right it would end that way.

"Oh, man, you kill me," said Cowboy. "How come you never go to school any more? You going to be the richest shoeshine man in Dogtown?"

"Well, you know how it is," Charlie said. "You cats haven't caught up with me yet. When there's something I want to know, I'll start coming again."

"If things get slow," Cowboy said, "I got another idea for you. Dance on street corners for nickels."

The others, except the West Indian boy, all laughed and looked at Charlie, waiting for his counterpunch. Charlie could taste his anger, bitter as pennies in his mouth. But he kept a grin pasted on.

"With big spenders like you around," he said, "I might make up to ten cents a day."

Cowboy jingled some coins in his pocket. "You making me sorry for you, Charlie. Maybe I'll throw a little business your way. I've got time for a shine before school. You're a real pro, what kinda shine you think I need?"

He stuck out one of his cowboy boots, displaying it for Charlie's professional opinion. It was short and black, and so tight that his toes bulged as though the boot were packed with walnuts.

Charlie felt his ears tighten like a spitting cat's, the way they did when his anger was past holding. But he recalled something Uncle Baron had told him once: *Anybody can get mad, Charlie. But the fella that gets mad is the one that gets hurt by the one that keeps his cool.* And right away he felt his brain cool down.

"I'll tell you what, Cowboy," he said soberly. "Those are real fine boots, in my opinion. Lemme see, here—" He knelt and tested the leather with his thumb, then rose. "Uh-*huh!* That's kangaroo hide. *Female* kangaroo, the best kind—cut from the kangaroo's pouch. Now, man, I was going to say an Inspection Shine, but I don't know. I think you've been waxing those boots a little heavy, and prob'ly only a Burn Shine would straighten them out."

A good feeling came over the group. Charlie saw even Caesar smiling, as though confident that his new friend was in charge now. Cowboy, however, went on guard.

"What's that-there Burn Shine?" he asked.

"Well, lemme explain it this way," Charlie said. "The wax has built up so that it's flaking off—you see? All of a sudden the whole uppers are going to flake off—a mess. Now, a Burn Shine melts off all the old wax. Then I build it up from the bottom so they're like new.—Here, I'll show you," he said.

Uncapping a bottle of alcohol, he soaked a cotton swab on a wire. He struck a match and lighted the swab, as the boys crowded closer. As the blue flame flickered, he put his foot up on a stool and rubbed the shoe with the swab. Where the flame passed, the wax flared up yellow, then burned out to gray leather. He puffed out the flame.

"Then," he said, "you do like this—" Into the bald stripe, he rubbed some black wax and brushed it to a shine. "Three coats, and they're like new. See?"

"Huh!" Cowboy was fascinated. "How much?"

"Eighty-five cents. To my friends, the price is sixty."

Cowboy hesitated. The others were saying, "Hey, how about that?" and, "He's right, Cowboy, that's what you need." Charlie kept a strictly business expression on his face, helping Cowboy to realize that if he backed down now, he would look both cheap and chicken.

At last Cowboy made a big-spender gesture and climbed up. Charlie dipped the swab again. He struck a paper match, and the alcohol burned cold-blue and yellow. With quick strokes, he burned off part of one boot before the swab began to go dry. Then he poured more alcohol onto the cotton. As the swab filled, burning alcohol suddenly flooded Cowboy's boot. In an instant the boot was ablaze.

Cowboy yelled, "Watch it, idiot!"

Charlie began muttering things. "Never done that before! Caesar, mahn, get me— Where's that fire extinguisher?"

Cowboy yelled as the heat burned through his shoes. He leaped to the floor and began trying to stamp out the flame. Everyone was shrieking with laughter. Cowboy attempted to pull off the boot, but burned his hands. All this time Charlie was muttering to himself as he hunted for the fire extinguisher.

"Man, I am *so* sorry! Just keep cool. Saw that extinguisher last week, so it's gotta be here—"

Finally, choking on his laughter, Charlie found the red CO_2 bottle on the wall and lifted it down. "Hold still, now!" he said. He pointed the black plastic nozzle at Cowboy's foot and squeezed the trigger. The parlor rocked to the hoarse bellow of gases. Snow and vapor engulfed Cowboy's legs.

In the rear, Leonard woke with a startled yell. As Charlie released the trigger, the snowstorm petered out. Frosty flakes clung to Cowboy's pants and legs. His right boot, stripped of wax, looked as though it had been boiled.

"Say, whaaat's goin' on?" Leonard asked, blinking in the doorway.

"This punk—this fink!" Cowboy choked. He started for Charlie with his fist cocked. Charlie fired the gun in his face. Cowboy vanished in the new snowstorm, reappearing with frosty hair and lashes.

Charlie spread his arms. "Man, I'm sorry! It was an accident. Leave the boots and I'll fix 'em."

Teary-eyed with laughter, the boys tugged at Cowboy's arm. "Gonna be late, Cowboy! Come on!" Caesar urged.

Cowboy stared furiously at Charlie, but with Leonard standing there and everyone pulling at him, he turned abruptly and walked away.

Chapter 5

Breathing Man

That wasn't like you, Charlie," Leonard said, as Charlie started putting things away. "I don't know what happened, but I got bad vibrations about it. Tell me, boy."

"He wanted a shine. I was giving him a Burn Shine."

Leonard suppressed a grin. "Well, next time," he said, "you give him a shine somewheres else. Soon as you've cleaned up, now, you'd better go to school."

"Okay," Charlie said humbly.

Leonard opened a couple of cokes. Charlie sat down to drink his, frowning.

"Leonard," he said, "I reckon I'll get out of this town."

"Now, Charlie, whatever it is, it'll pass. Your mama and daddy need you."

"I don't need my old man, though. And I've got to make some bread to take off with. Gonna find my Uncle Baron."

"He's one right nice fella, ain't he? Well, maybe it

would be a good idea for a while. Got any traveling money?"

"No. That's why I'm telling you. Where can a kid make some big money quick?"

"Why don't you talk to Breathing Man? He's got along for fifteen years without working. He should know an angle or two."

"Say, he might! Thanks, I will."

Years before, Breathing Man had had a seizure of some sort that had given him quite a scare. Now he slept in a chair, afraid to lie down, since people died in bed. And he was possessed of the curious idea that his breathing apparatus had been altered by his seizure, so that it no longer worked automatically. He had to keep thinking,

Breathe in. Breathe out. Breathe in . . .

He spent his days around the Hob Nob Pool Hall, hearing and knowing everything about Dogtown, and tending to his breathing.

Just as Charlie was about to leave the shoeshine stand for school, his father appeared. He was wearing a coat, as though coming from work. Though he did not smile, he looked pleasant. In his hand he held a postcard.

"Hello, Clark," he said to Leonard. "How's it with you?"

"Oh, you know," Leonard chuckled.

"Just got home," Roscoe Matthews said to Charlie, "and I found this postcard. It's from your Uncle Baron. It was wrote three weeks ago, but he had the wrong address. Says he's coming to pass a few days with us as soon as some racetrack closes. That was day before yesterday, so he ought to be dropping in any time now."

Excitement seized Charlie. "No kidding!"

Roscoe Matthews said casually, "Why don't you keep what you earn today, Chahles? Get a present for your uncle."

"Fine," Charlie said.

What's got into him? Charlie wondered, as his father walked off. Maybe his mother had told him what Charlie had said about going away with Uncle Baron, and he wanted to sweeten up Uncle Baron to make sure the deal went through.

When his father was out of sight, Charlie headed for school, rolling his shoulders and ducking his head like a boxer, feeling strong and confident. Uncle Baron coming! In two weeks, give or take a couple of days, the two of them would be taking off together! In the meantime, it was important to scratch up some money, so that he could say, cool as a mile of wet wash:

"By the way, Uncle Baron, here's fifty dollars. It'll pay my expenses till the money's coming in."

Before he knew it, he was nearing Sam's Hob Nob

Pool Hall, where Breathing Man hung out. There, sunning himself like a lizard in a chair propped against the brick wall, sat Breathing Man. The bricks were crumbly, stained from an old fire, with a narrow door through which customers came and went. To the right of the door was a greasy window behind which was a tiny kitchen where hot dogs and tacos were concocted. Breathing Man's eyes were closed. Winter and summer, he wore a long Army overcoat, with a muffler around his neck and a knitted GI cap on his head. He took no chances with his health.

"Hello, Breathing Man," Charlie said cheerfully.

Breathing Man opened his eyes, smiled, and stirred a little. "Hello, Charlie," he said.

"How's your health?" Charlie asked.

"Why, I guess passable."

With a quarter, Charlie tapped on the kitchen window. "I'm going to have a hot dog," he said. "How about you? I'm buying. My uncle's in town and I'm celebrating."

"Well, now, I might have one."

Sam came to the window. Charlie ordered two foot-long hot dogs drenched with red chili. They ate, chatting, while Charlie squatted against the wall.

"Say, Breathing Man," Charlie said, "if you wanted to make some loot fast, how would you go about it? I mean, where's it buried in this end of town?"

Breathing Man

Breathing Man turned his head. His dusty walnut face beamed at Charlie.

"I'd open a vein. And sell the blood."

"No, I mean, really—"

"I sell lots of blood. The plasma center. Five dollar's a smash. Ninety-six and Archer."

Charlie brightened. "Hey! How much will they buy at a time?"

"Don't know. They takes a bottleful. Then you go to another center. But it's dangerous to sell too much."

Charlie imagined himself writing it down in the diary he sometimes kept: *Sold blood at Plasma Center. $5 a smash.*

"Great. Anything else?"

"Find things. Alleys. Vacant lots."

"You mean like money? And watches and stuff?"

"A few coins. Coke bottles. Odds and ends."

"Is that how you make a living?"

"Soldier's pension. Bakeries give me nice things. And restaurants." Breathing Man chuckled. "And folks buys me hot dogs."

Charlie laughed. He rose. "Keep thinking about it, will you? I've got to make a stake to go away with my Uncle Baron."

Breathing Man closed his eyes and did not speak. In a slow, even rhythm, he had got back to the business of breathing.

Charlie was fifteen minutes late for Sheet Metal. After that came Gym, then English. Mr. Toia's English class was preparing to act out a play called *Raisin in the Sun.* There were too few parts to go around, so they drew straws to see who read and who merely followed in the book. A girl named Gale drew the part of the grandmother, and Mr. Toia asked another girl to be Ruth, her daughter. Charlie won the role of the husband.

He bent over the magazine in which the play was printed, skimming ahead, fascinated by this story of Negroes trying to get out of a Chicago slum. The play pulled him under like quicksand. It was salted with the sad and funny truths of life.

I could write a play like this! he thought. *People would read it and think, "That is so true. That is just how it is."*

At the end, when the man whom the husband had trusted with his money had run off with it, the whole class was angry. Some of them said it was stupid to end a play like that.

"Why shouldn't it end that way?" Mr. Toia asked. "Isn't that the way a lot of things end? Maybe the author was trying to tell us something. What do you think she was trying to tell us, Cowboy?"

"Don't trust nobody," Cowboy said. "That husband was so dumb."

Mr. Toia squinted one eye. "Or maybe Mrs.

Mr. Toia

Hansberry was saying that no matter how bad a situation is, we've got to look it in the eye, and not try to solve our problems by daydreaming and gambling. Charlie, what do you say?"

"The husband was stupid," Charlie said, surprised at the upwelling of anger in him. "You've got to trust people sometimes, but he was stupid to trust that guy so far."

It was a good play, but it left a bad feeling in him. When people needed something as bad as those people did, then things should work out, he felt.

He got out of sight as soon as school ended. Not that he was afraid of Cowboy, but he might as well give him a chance to cool off, and to realize that he had asked for it. He considered taking a bus uptown to sell some blood, but decided it would keep in his veins until Saturday. Better to go back to the shine stand and get some of the late-afternoon action.

Sauntering along, he spun himself a yarn about how it would be when Uncle Baron arrived: "*My, you've grown a foot!*" his uncle would say, and Charlie would say, "*Big enough to spell you on the driving, I bet. Can I go with you?*"

An old Volkswagen bus was parked near the shine parlor. The body was painted a chalky blue. It had Kentucky license plates, was rusty, dusty, and dented like an old tin can. The windows were curtained with red-and-white material like a tablecloth.

Battered though it was, the bus had a snug look, and he wondered how much a little old car like that would cost. Be just right for a boy to live in while he went to college.

He passed it, and was just entering the shine parlor when a door of the bus creaked and a man called out:

"Hey there, young fella!"

He turned in surprise, and saw Uncle Baron climbing out.

Chapter 6

Mayor Charlie

Charlie did not know whether to kiss his uncle's cheek, as he used to, or to shake hands. Uncle Baron took Charlie's hand in both of his own and nearly crushed it. He was a chunky man with Charlie's own strong build and much of Charlie's look in his face, from his mother's side of the family. His clothes said "racetrack"—a gray-checked suit, yellow shirt, and blue tie.

"We just got your card," Charlie said. "How long are you going to stay?"

"Till the money runs out. How's your folks? I haven't gone there yet because I didn't want to wake up your dad. Is he still working nights?"

"Yes. You've got a new car, huh?"

"New to me. Look inside. I live in it!"

He swung the side doors open, and Charlie looked in. There were a bed, a tiny stove and icebox, and a little closet. It was like a doll's house.

"Done the cabinetwork myself. I'm real proud of them mitered corners. And there's a little tent rig I can set up beside the car for more room. The bed folds up into a seat, and I can carry six people."

Charlie almost blurted "Take me with you!" There was glamour even in the dust on the car and the few wisps of hay on the floor. They told of faroff places, of excitement and big money.

Baron drew a gold watch from a vest pocket and raised a lid on it. "Four ten," he said. "I've got to run over and see a man about a little deal, Charlie. Tell your mother not to cook supper—I'll bring something so's she won't have to cook tonight."

"What kind of a deal?" Charlie asked. "Are you buying a horse?"

Uncle Baron patted his shoulder. "No, no. My life ain't all bangtails. I got lots of irons in the fire. Had a little correspondence with this guy, and I think we can do some business. If we do, I stand to make a pot of money."

Uncle Baron brought hamburger, buns, and crackling bags of potato chips. While Buster crawled all over him, puppy-like, he dug a small barbecue hole in the back yard near a tattered banana plant. In it he built a fire of kindling, and carried a sooty piece of chain-link fencing from his bus and laid it across the hole. Then he put hamburgers to broil on the grill.

Neighbors on the north and south gazed over the wooden fence and said howdy to Uncle Baron, while

Uncle Baron

sniffing the fragrance of the broiling meat. Charlie knew they would have been pleased to join the party, but no one suggested it.

As night came, they sat around on kitchen chairs, blinking at the smoke, and talking.

"Sometimes I wisht we was back on the farm in Georgy," Charlie's mother said. "It was hard, but there was good times, too. Here's it's all hard work and no good feelings."

Uncle Baron wagged his head. "I been in Georgy since you have, Sis. It ain't all good times, I'll tell you that. It's muling along on a couple of dollars a day and all the chiggers you can scratch. Chillun with swollen bellies, and shacks the wind rattles like dice."

"There's swollen bellies and rundown shacks in this part of the world, too," said Charlie's dad.

They talked on, grownup talk. As the sky darkened, firelight brushed the tiny yard with magic. In Charlie's imagination, the overgrown plants became jungle trees. Squinting his eyes, he slipped into a reverie:

". . . Charlie," said the President of Mexico, "you can turn me down if you want to. I wouldn't blame you. But there is this village back in the mountains that needs help. The people don't trust Mexicans or white men, but they might let a Negro help them. There's a lot of sick children, and their

crops are so puny the people are half starved. If you'd be willing to go in there—"

By night, Charlie drove up through jungly mountains to the village. He camped in the plaza while the people slept. In the dusty little blue bus he drove, he carried things like rifles, toys, medicines, sacks of beans, and seeds. In the morning, the people found him camped there in the plaza.

"Who are you, hombre?" they asked. They were Indians wearing white clothes like pajamas, and they looked mighty sour and dangerous.

"My name is Carlos Matthews," said Charlie. "I'm here to help you."

There was a very sick child in the village. Don Carlos used his medicines on him, and he got well. Right away the people began to trust him. They let him help them in other ways. They gave him some land to farm so that he would not leave. His seeds made such wonderful crops that they all wanted to use them. He healed the sick, settled legal matters, and every boy child that was born was named Carlos. They elected Charlie mayor and called him, El Gran Carlos—Big Charlie.

"What kinda business was this you had today?" the voice of Charlie's father asked.

Blinking, Charlie reeled back from his reverie. In fact, he realized sheepishly, he had been sound asleep. He was sitting cross-legged in front of Uncle

Baron, whose hand lay on his shoulder, steadying him so that he would not pitch face-forward into the fire.

"Oh, just a little deal with a man I met last year," said Uncle Baron.

"What kinda deal?" insisted Charlie's dad.

"I'd rather not say, Roscoe. It's been my experience that you can spoil a thing by mouthing it up too much. But this one's red-hot."

Charlie's ears pricked up.

"If it's so good," said Charlie's mother, "how come he don't keep it himself?"

"He's more of an idea man than a doer. He's got the merchandise, but he don't know how to use it. *I* know how to use it, but I haven't got the cash to buy it from him."

As they ate the hamburgers, drank soft drinks and beer, and crunched through bag after bag of potato chips, Charlie's face grew hot with excitement. For suddenly he knew how he was going to sell himself to his uncle! Uncle Baron needed money. Charlie was going to shake this town by its heels till all the loose cash fell out of its pockets, and buy in with him.

As the red coals in the fire hole faded under gray ash, Charlie's mother said: "You kids stir yourselves, now. Take your dirty plates inside and get ready for bed."

"Tell you what, Baron," said Roscoe Matthews.

"I'll tear out some of the fence here and y'all can drive in from the alley. You'll have peace and quiet, without some cop waking you up every ten minutes to look at your engine number."

Charlie and his father went to work ripping out a section of the low picket fence that had curled itself around like dried leather. Then they stamped the weeds and dusty geraniums flat. Down the alley came the little bus. Uncle Baron tooled it into the yard, parking neatly, with the bumper nudging the back wall of the kitchen. The branches of an old camphor tree drooped over it. Uncle Baron turned on the dome lights, and Charlie grinned with delight. It was exactly like a tiny house—bed, stove, cupboards.

. . . *Me and Uncle Baron—all over the country!* he thought.

His father went to the house.

"Get in. Try the bed," Uncle Baron invited Charlie.

The narrow bed ran fore and aft. Charlie stretched out, then flipped over on his stomach. The light burned above his head, a perfect place to read. As surely as the Wise Men had known that the star was leading them somewhere, Charlie knew that his life and his uncle's were meshing like gear teeth. It was certainly more than accident that, hours after he had made up his mind to find Uncle Baron, here his uncle had come driving in!

Uncle Baron lighted a cigar. "You getting to be quite a boy," he said. "Be a big man when you get your growth."

"Big enough to do a day's work now."

"Bet you are."

Charlie's heart began to pump. He wanted to phrase his plea in such a way that it would be hard for his uncle to refuse him. Yet he could not find the words. Finally he blurted:

"Can I go with you?"

In surprise, Uncle Baron took the cigar out of his mouth. "Huh? Go where?"

"Wherever you go! I could spell you on the driving. I could help cook, and—and—"

Embarrassed, his uncle scratched an eyebrow with a thumbnail. "Reckon you could, Charlie, but you know how it is. I don't make the kind of money to take care of you. And I never stay in one place long enough for you to go to school—"

"School doesn't matter. As far as money goes, I could scare up little jobs and make money. I'm strong. I could help you haul hay and—"

"Charlie-boy, I wouldn't knock your talents, but I ain't sure you could carry your weight."

"Yes, I could!"

"Maybeso, but I can't gamble on us getting stranded somewhere."

"What if I had some money to start with?

Couldn't I kinda buy in? You said you needed cash for that deal."

His uncle gazed down the rows of mournful shacks lining the alley. "If you could make money in Dogtown, Charlie, I reckon you could make money anywheres. But—"

"How much do you need for that investment?"

Uncle Baron smiled, and patted Charlie's hand. Finally he said, "It goes about like this: For a hundred and seventy-five dollars' cash, I could own the thing clean."

Charlie's mind plunged along. "How long will you be here?" he asked.

"I could stay a couple of weeks if I had a reason."

"What if I made that much money? Couldn't we go partners on this deal, and I'd go with you when you leave?"

Uncle Baron thought for a long time. "Why, I reckon that'd be up to your folks," he said. "We could try it for a while, if they said so."

Charlie bumped his head on the roof as he piled off the bed. Jumping from the bus, he collided with a man standing there in the darkness.

"Slow down!" It was his father.

"Dad! Uncle Baron says—"

His father was carrying two cans of beer. He handed one to Baron, and drank from the other.

"I heard what he said. I been standing here a

while. Shoot, if he can stand you, I reckon there's no harm in it. If you don't make enough to send anything home, at least you won't be eating us into the po'house here."

Chapter 7

A Fortune in Bedsprings

Daylight was slanting through the window when Charlie opened his eyes. For a few instants the wheels in his head did not turn. Then they spun, and his mind was racing again. He rolled out of the covers with a murmur of delight.

Day One in his new life!

Buster, wakened by the sounds of his brother dressing, gazed out of a heap of rumpled bedclothes. "Whatcha doin', Charlie? Isn't it Saturday?"

"Gotta hustle," Charlie said.

No one else was up in the small house. It was everyone's day off but Charlie's. Pushing a stray cat off the doorstep, he stole out to make sure he had not merely dreamed that there was a blue bus in the back yard. But it was there, and from the curtained interior came a gentle snore. Charlie returned to the kitchen and found breakfast food and milk.

One month to make a hundred and seventy-five dollars!

Impossible. There were grown men in Dogtown who did not make that kind of money—did not make *any* money. But he shut the door on doubt and piled the furniture against it. It was not a question of *whether* he would make it, but of *how*.

At eight forty-five he came dogtrotting up to the shine parlor. Leonard was there with the West Indian kid Caesar. As Charlie entered, Caesar grinned and said hello. Leonard, working on a pair of black-and-white ladies' shoes, nodded at Charlie.

"Right on time, Charlie. You fellas know each other, don't you?"

They said they did. A customer came in, then another. While Charlie and Leonard shined their shoes, Caesar sat quietly in the corner tapping rhythm on a bucket. After the customers left, Charlie told Leonard about Uncle Baron.

"Well, ain't that nice!" Leonard said. "Now all you need is a hundred and seventy-five bucks. If you pull that off, you might try walking on water."

"Breathing Man gave me some angles."

Two men stopped before the shine stand. Both were white, overweight but hard-looking, as though they had been stamped out of the same kind of tough dough. Charlie recalled seeing one of the men in Dogtown before, a heavy-bellied man with longish chestnut hair and a complexion like tallow. He wore the somber expression of a man thinking about his troubles. The men walked inside. The smell of liquor blended with that of shoe polish.

"Yes, sir!" Leonard said. "How are you today, Mr. Ellis?"

"Okay, Leonard, how you doing?" said the man with the chestnut hair. "This is Mr. Woodson, my partner."

Leonard shook hands with Mr. Woodson.

As he worked, Charlie was conscious of Woodson's scrutiny. One of his eyes was permanently cocked, as though a deep distrust of the human race had lodged in that one eye. Another man drifted in, and Caesar got to work on his shoes.

"Woodson bought in with me on those rentals I have over on Seneca Street," Ellis told Leonard, fitting a cigarette into a plastic holder. "He's a fight promoter, too."

"Is that a fact?" Leonard said.

"You kids ever do any fighting?" asked Woodson.

"Just enough to get by," said Charlie.

Woodson reached down and squeezed Charlie's shoulder. Unexpectedly, he raked a fast hook at his chin. Charlie's head rolled and the punch grazed him. He blinked in surprise. Woodson chuckled. Then, "How about you, Shorty?" he asked Caesar. "You interested in fighting?"

Caesar shook his head. "With legs like mine, you don't have to fight. You can run."

"How tall are you?"

"Six-five."

"How about you?" Woodson asked Charlie.

"Five-nine."

Woodson chuckled. "You know what'd make a good freak match?" he said to his partner. "A match between a couple of kids like these. The less they knew about boxing, the better."

Ellis nodded. "How about it for some Friday night? Battle royal—the hell with the rule book, and fifty dollars to the winner!"

Charlie considered it. He had never seen fifty dollars that was not nailed down so hard you broke all your nails trying to get it up. *Watch out*, he told himself.

"What do you say?" Woodson said.

"I guess not," Charlie told him.

"Seventy-five dollars?"

"Nope," Charlie said. Caesar shook his head too.

"What's the matter? Anything wrong with our money?"

Working with the brushes, Charlie said: "No, sir. But we only fight for pleasure. Did you say you've got some rentals around here? Maybe there's some work I could do for you."

Ellis looked at him. He blew smoke between them. "Well, I might have. How about a treasure hunt?"

"*Treasure* hunt?"

"You might strike it big. Might only make day wages."

Charlie was skeptical. "What kind of treasure?"

Ellis winked. "That's the thing about treasure hunts—you never know what you're going to find. Know that reservoir at the top of Seneca Street?"

"Sure."

"Show up there at four o'clock, if you're interested."

"Is there enough treasure for two guys?" Caesar asked hopefully.

"There is if you're not too greedy."

"I'm greedy," Charlie said. "We'd better wait till we see it."

When the men left, each paid a dollar for his shine.

"What do you know about those dudes, Leonard?" Charlie asked.

Leonard said: "All's I know is Mr. Ellis owns a lot of slum houses. He's what they calls a slum lord. But there's plenty more dollars where these came from. Treasure, though—I don't know. If there's any treasure in Dogtown, I been going around with my eyes closed."

Charlie mulled over Ellis's offer, sawed between the fear of making a fool of himself and hating to miss out on a fast dollar in the home town of the slow buck. Leonard was out back watching some men shoot craps on his kitchen table. Through the partly closed door Charlie could see them rolling a pair of pink dice, each one no bigger than half of an aspirin.

"What do you think?" he asked Caesar.

"Worth looking into, mahn," Caesar said. "And if there's enough work, it'd go a lot faster for you with a buddy, right?"

"Maybe," Charlie hedged.

He went next door to the liquor store and called home. In a moment, Uncle Baron came on the line.

"Can you drive down?" Charlie asked him. "I want you to eyeball a deal for me."

"Why, sure. We're pardners, ain't we?"

In a few minutes the bus pulled up. Charlie introduced Caesar to Uncle Baron. Then the boys climbed up onto the high, hard seat of the car. "Make a U and go south," Charlie said. After a few blocks, the bars and stores gave way to vacant lots, half-demolished buildings, and used-car lots.

"Turn right at that church," Charlie said.

Uncle Baron downshifted, and the bus howled up a side street. Seneca Street sloped uphill for one block and ended at a chain-link fence. Beyond the fence, a roofed reservoir was tucked into the flank of the hill. As a child, Charlie had climbed the fence many times to crawl about the roof of the concrete tank and stare fearfully through cracks at the dark shine of still water. The bus labored up between old frame houses jumbled together. Rising crookedly among them were telephone poles, TV antennas, and skinny palm trees with brown pelts of dead branches hanging down. Overturned wheel toys were everywhere. Children playing in the street got out of the way with screeches as the bus ground up the hill.

"Treasure?" Uncle Baron said dubiously, eyeing the neighborhood. "I don't know about you, boy."

Charlie, too, was growing uneasy. He had forgotten how mean the neighborhood was over here. Most of the houses looked as though they had a skin disease, with dry scabs of paint flaking off their warped siding. The bigger houses sheltered three or four families. Probably no one knew how many children lived on Seneca Street, any more than they could calculate the number of roaches. They were just part of the wildlife.

"Must be the gentlemen's Caddy parked yonder," Charlie's uncle said.

At the top of the street, on the right, a gunmetal-colored Cadillac convertible was parked before a vacant lot. Standing near a mellow old brick wall were Ellis and his partner. Charlie was reminded of a pair of soldiers in no-man's-land, for the treasure site resembled a morsel of a battlefield picked up by a steam shovel and deposited here in heaps and drifts. Perhaps a house had stood here at one time.

There seemed to be the memory of one in the scraps of plaster, heaps of tar paper, and wistful remnants of a garden—bright-green-and-bronze castor-bean tangles and dusty rice-paper plants. The smoky sun glancing over the hills caught glints of glass everywhere. Rotting tires and auto parts thrust out of mounds of trash.

Charlie's mouth pulled down. "I'll tell them it's no deal," he said.

"No. Long as we're here, let's talk to them," said Uncle Baron.

The men waited by the wall, which was about four feet high, looking at an old steering wheel Woodson held in his hands. Clambering through hummocks of earth and trash, Charlie, Caesar, and Uncle Baron went to the rear of the lot to talk to them. Charlie saw a rat poke its whiskered nose from under an overturned baby buggy and duck back.

Ellis's pouched eyes appraised them. "I see you brought your business manager," he said to Charlie, with a wink.

"This is my uncle," Charlie said.

Uncle Baron said smoothly, "The boy tells me you were talking about a deal of some kind, gem'men."

Ellis took the old steering wheel from his partner's hands. "Ever see one of these? Magnesium spokes and walnut rim! A classic, and in good shape."

Good or bad shape, Charlie decided, it was still junk.

Then Ellis turned to the brick wall and worked a top brick free of the grip of crumbly mortar. The brick was a rosy color, flecked with particles of cement.

"Guess what this brick is worth," he said.

"As a guess—zero," said Uncle Baron.

"Fifteen cents! Used brick brings a better price than new brick. I was offered a hundred dollars for that wall, once."

"I see," Uncle Baron said. "You owns this lot, then?"

"The whole block. The City wants us to clean the lot off. I could have it bulldozed off for a hundred, but why do that when I can get it done for nothing?"

"How you gonna get it done for nothing?"

Ellis silently handed a business card to Uncle Baron, who squinted at it, then passed it to Charlie. "Can't read a thing without my specs."

Or with, Charlie thought, for the fact was that Uncle Baron's love affair with education had been only a summer's madness. He was practically illiterate, and the postcards he sent were always written in a different hand, depending on whom he had got to write them for him.

" 'Ideal Junk & Refuse,' " Charlie read aloud. " 'Harry Egig—' "

"Egigian," said Ellis. "A junk dealer. He'll clean the lot for nothing."

"Then why mess around with a couple of kids?"

"Because Harry'd do a sloppy job, unless I stayed on his neck. Plus the fact that these boys tell me they're trying to make some money. It's good sense to keep the business in the neighborhood, isn't it?"

Uncle Baron rubbed his chin. "What kinda deal are we talking about, exactly?" he asked.

"I've got ten days to clean the lot. You'd deliver it clean, and own anything you turned up in the process."

Uncle Baron shook his head. "Well, I don't know—"

Ellis said impatiently: "Man, every bottle you haul to the winery is worth a penny! And look at that heap of copper tubing over by the bathtub. That's *cash,* friend. Plus, they used to have a little auto-wrecking operation here. There's hundreds of old headlights and Lord knows what buried under the junk. Classic car parts! Some wrecking lot would pay a fortune for the stuff."

Another rat poked its head out to give them a hard woman-next-door stare. Charlie said:

"How much are rats worth? It'd be between them and us for the junk."

"Two bits apiece, boy. That's the new City bounty on rodents."

Uncle Baron began sauntering through the refuse like a plantation overseer. Charlie started counting wine bottles, and Caesar estimated the number of bricks in the wall.

Uncle Baron said doubtfully: "I'd have to have it in writing, Mr. Ellis. Don't want the law rousting me for trespass."

Ellis whipped out a typewritten paper. "Naturally. This is just an informal agreement. I've put in a penalty clause of $50 in case you walk out without finishing the job. That's only half what it would cost me to have the job finished."

"Lemme just look this over," Uncle Baron said. "Boys, come along to the bus."

He laid the paper on a small table bolted to the wall of the bus. Charlie and Caesar read the paper together. It sounded all right to Charlie.

But Caesar asked: "What about that fifty bucks? Would they try to collect it if we finished the work?"

"No, sir, because I ain't going to be around long enough to get stung, if they do get nasty."

"Then it looks to me," Caesar said, "like there might be some money in it. There's at least three hundred bricks alone." He glanced at Charlie. "You're going to need help, though, mahn, making bricks out of a brick wall."

"Stop hounding me," Charlie said. "You're in."

Uncle Baron held the paper up to the light as if something important were written on it in invisible ink. "Any way you look at it," he said, "we're buying a junk and diamond mine, and there's going to be a lot more junk than diamonds. We'll pick out the diamonds, then rent a 'dozer and finish the job. Only thing that bothers me is the time. If you boys can't start work till after school, I'll be gray-haired and on two canes before we finish."

"No sweat," Charlie said. "I'm on a leave of absence."

Caesar hesitated. "My father would skin me if I ditched. But I'll really make the dirt fly from three thirty to six."

Uncle Baron scratched his head some more, and finally said that would be all right, but since Caesar would be putting in less time, he would have to settle for less money—say a quarter of the take. Caesar agreed. They shook hands on it, and Uncle Baron found a pencil stub, licked it, and signed the paper.

They went back and shook hands with Woodson and Ellis. The men drove off. The boys and Uncle Baron roamed the lot a while longer. Charlie felt differently about the lot now, as though he somehow owned it, like a miner who had himself a claim and was going to work it for gold. Every time a rat poked its snout from a hole to glare at him, a cash register in his head tinkled and rang up twenty-five cents; even the bottles shone like new pennies.

Chapter 8

Rat Pack

The next day, Sunday, they drove over to the lot so early the grass was still drenched with dew. Buster and Callie went along. Caesar was sitting on the wall, waiting. While he and Charlie got to work on the bricks, using a hammer and cold chisel to loosen them, the younger kids started searching for bottles and metal. Uncle Baron prospected for usable car parts.

No one on Seneca Street seemed to have anything better to do than to stand around and ask what they were doing. Once Charlie looked up to see a swarm of children crawling around in the bus. He locked it up; then it was a fight to keep them off the roof.

By evening Charlie knew several things about bricks.

In the first place, there were over two thousand of them.

Every third brick would break in handling.

Bricks and mortar wore out a pair of cheap cotton gloves in a half hour, then went to work wearing out skin.

Buster and Callie collected nearly a hundred wine bottles. Uncle Baron shot seven rats with an old .22-caliber rifle he kept in the bus. He put them in a lard can and kept them in the shade.

"Yes, sir," he said, as they drove home, "this here looks like a going business. Tomorrow I'll load up with samples and find the best places to sell our junk."

Monday morning, before breakfast, Charlie hurried to the shine stand to tell Leonard how things stood. "I'll get you a boy to take my place," he said. "If things work out, I won't be coming back. But if anything goes wrong I'd sure like to have my job back."

Leonard said it would be all right.

Charlie ran down to the Hob Nob and asked Breathing Man about a replacement for him. Breathing Man said there were several boys who hung around the pool hall most of the time, and he suggested Curtis Lloyd as a steady worker who would be worth the money Leonard paid him. He promised to send him down to the shine stand the first time he saw him.

Charlie loped home in time for breakfast. Afterward, he and Uncle Baron took off for the lot. Dogtown was still uncoiling like a chilled snake, its bums scratching in doorways and its jobless men standing on certain street corners that were supposed to be good luck for pick-and-shovel workers.

They parked, pulled on what was left of their gloves, and picked their way to the wall, where they had left the samples.

Suddenly Uncle Baron halted, staring. "What's gone on here?" he growled.

Charlie looked, and choked on fury. All the bottles they had collected had been hurled against the wall. The copper and brass were gone. The lard can of rats had vanished.

"That bum!" he said furiously. "It was Cowboy."

"What's this?" Uncle Baron said. A tiny wooden cross made of two sticks had been thrust into the earth near the wall. Charlie bent to read what had been penciled on the crossbar.

" 'Here Lies a Dirty Rat,' " he read.

Using the cross as a trowel, he dug away some earth and exposed the bodies of several of their rats. "That clown!" he snarled. "I'll bury him when I catch him."

Uncle Baron looked around, hands in his pockets. "At least he left the bricks, and they're all that was worth much."

They scrounged up some more bottles and copper, cleaned up the rats, and loaded everything into the bus. "If I ain't back by six," said Uncle Baron, "you'd better figure on walking home. No telling how far I'll have to go to make my contacts."

Charlie burned his anger out in hard work. Soon it grew lonesome. He was glad for the small children who roamed about picking things up and dropping them. He realized the lot was their playground. He settled their squabbles. He gave them interesting bits of junk to keep them out of his hair.

At noon he ate a peanut-butter sandwich and drank a warm coke. Lying on his back on the ground, he watched birds paddle across the blue ocean of the sky. As he listened to the voices of Dogtown, a small motorcycle came snorting up the street. He raised his head.

Mr. Toia, parking, waved at him.

Now, what? Charlie wondered. He had thought things were settled as far as school went. Carrying a brown paper bag, Mr. Toia weaved through the heaps of junk to the wall.

"Hi, Charlie," he said. "I didn't have Playground, so I thought I'd join you for lunch."

"How'd you know I was here?"

"Caesar told me."

They ate, discussing Charlie's plans.

"I've got to get out of this mess," Charlie said. "Maybe I'll go to night school after I leave here."

"Oh, no doubt," said the teacher cheerfully. "I think you'll probably wind up as the brightest man on some garbage truck."

"No, man," Charlie insisted. "I'll have more chance with my uncle than I will with my old man."

Unpersuaded, Mr. Toia smiled. "Who's going to hold the money you make?" he asked.

"My uncle, I guess."

"I'll tell you how it is with money," said Mr. Toia. "It leaks away like air out of a punctured tire unless you put it where you can't get at it. If you want, I'll be glad to hold the stakes for you."

For an instant Charlie considered whether this might be some sort of teacherly plot to stall him in Dogtown forever. But no, Mr. Toia wasn't that mean. Charlie rubbed two bricks together, working off the mortar.

"How would that work?" he asked.

"I'd keep the money in the principal's office for you. When you wanted it, you could say the word and I'd get it for you. That way no sneak thief would get it, and nothing else would happen to it."

Charlie nodded. "That's good. I don't know how I'd get it to you, though. If I showed up at school—"

"That's right," Mr. Toia said. "Why don't you leave it at Leonard's, and I'll pick it up every morning on the way to school? I'll leave a receipt each time."

"Fine. Thanks," Charlie said. "Thanks a lot. I really mean it about night school, Mr. Toia," he added.

"Sure you do," the teacher said. "Lots of luck, Charlie."

Chapter 9

Finders Keepers

When Caesar finally arrived, he got straight to work as though perspiration might go out of style before dark. The two of them made a big hole in the wall. Whenever a rat showed its head one of them would snatch up the rifle and knock it off. Resting from brickwork, they turned up some hub caps, a couple of dozen wine bottles, and two automobile generators that might have a little value. The sun sank behind the reservoir, and the sky darkened to the color of crankcase drainings.

Charlie found a soggy doll. Tired, he sat on the wall and looked at it. It had no hair or lashes, but its eyes were bright blue. It put him in mind of an old woman who had been beautiful and thought she still was.

"Charlie," the old lady said to him, "you're the only person in this town who doesn't make fun of me. People say I'm crazy and live in a haunted house. But you do nice things for me and don't laugh at me."

Charlie mowed her lawn every week, and did

other things. She would give him a half dollar sometimes; not much, but he figured she could not afford any more than that. Then one day she called him into the house. She was holding a doll, and looked very sad.

"The doctor says I haven't got over a month to live, Charlie," she told him. "I'm all alone, and I don't mind dying. But I want to give this to you because you've been good to me."

Charlie took the doll so that her feelings would not be hurt. The day the old lady died, he got it out and looked at it. It was old and rotting. He decided to throw it away. But when he threw it into the trash barrel, the head broke, and out poured a handful of diamonds, rubies, and emeralds!

"Ouch!" someone called, breaking his fantasy. Charlie came blinking back to life to see Caesar standing in the middle of the darkening lot.

"What's the matter?" Charlie called.

"I stubbed my toe on something. It looks like a chunk of bronze or iron."

"Prob'ly a safe full of money," Charlie said. He joined him, and with scraps of metal they dug it up. What Caesar had stumbled on was a long metal box, badly corroded but still wearing patches of black paint.

"Strongbox, maybe!" Caesar said.

"No, it's more likely a Mickey Mouse lunchbox with the original sandwich," Charlie suggested.

The box, however, was as solid as stone. They turned it over. "Hey!" Charlie exclaimed. "It's a pay phone!"

The telephone was of a very old type, the cord rotted away and the receiver a truncated cone that you held to your ear. He had seen telephones just like it in gangster movies.

He put the receiver to his ear and spoke into the mouthpiece. "Hello, Cowboy? I forgot to tell you there's a guar'ntee on that Burn Shine. Drop in any old time and I'll touch 'em up for you."

Caesar chuckled. "Somebody must've stolen it out of a phone booth," he said. "Then he got the money out and dumped it here."

"But the lock isn't broken," Charlie pointed out. "Maybe he had to get rid of it in a hurry."

When he shook the telephone, there was a dull rattle of coins. Caesar scrambled back to the wall and got a screwdriver. By the time he returned, Charlie had broken into the money box with a piece of concrete. They spread a piece of tar paper on the ground, and in the cold, smoggy dusk shook out the coins. Some were welded together by corrosion; most of them, however, were in surprisingly good condition.

"I hardly ever saw any quarters like these," said Charlie. "They must be pretty old. I don't know how old the phone is, but it doesn't even have a dial."

They placed some more calls, giggling, then

counted the money. There was nine dollars and seventy-five cents! They picked through the coins, squinting at them in the dark. Nearly all the nickels had buffaloes and Indians on them, and the dimes bore a woman's head, not Mr. Roosevelt's.

Caesar rose to his knees. "Somebody coming!" he whispered.

Charlie saw shapes plodding from a back street toward the hole they had chipped in the wall. "Come on!" He crawled to the wall, then lay on the ground with Caesar near him. One by one, four boys stepped through the hole in the wall. The first wore a cowboy hat pinned up in front. Stopping near the pile of cleaned bricks, he gazed around, hands on hips. He swore.

"I was sure that stud would be here," he said. "Gonna be the sorriest day in his life when I catch him."

"Let's bust the bricks," said another.

"No—light a match first," Cowboy said. "Let's see what they did this time."

Charlie lay still. The odds were too bad to go looking for trouble. A match was scratched against a brick, and the flame burned a hole in the darkness. The boys plodded around.

"Hot dog!" one boy said. "Look here—"

He picked up the telephone. In a moment, Charlie knew, they would find the coins. He punched Caesar's arm, then got to his feet.

"Hey, Cowboy!" he called. "Looks like you caught up with me, man. How about a shine?"

He heard Cowboy grunt in surprise as the boys turned to stare at them.

"You the fink that stole our copper last night?" Charlie asked, starting toward Cowboy.

Cowboy lifted his hat and reset it over his eyes. "Never stole nothin'," he said. "This is just a vacant lot, ain't it?"

"But we got salvage rights on it, man. You busted our bottles and stole our scrap metal. You're a dirty fink."

Caesar was standing beside him now, a head taller than anyone there. As yet, no one showed any desire to jump them.

"What about my boots?" Cowboy challenged. "You ruined 'em."

"I told you I'd fix 'em."

"You can't never fix 'em like they were," said Cowboy. "So it's finders keepers on your lot." He leaned over to pick up the telephone.

Charlie thought fast and hard. Nobody ever really wanted to get messed up, and the two of them might be about evenly matched, which would mean some bent noses.

"Fair enough, Cowboy," he said. "I won the last match, you win this one. Keep the phone and we're square."

Cowboy handed the phone to the boy nearest him.

"Hold this," he said. "I'm going to give Chicken Charlie a tip for that shine, now—" He tossed his hat onto the ground.

Smack!

Cowboy stumbled back and sat down in a pile of laths. He made gasping sounds. Charlie had hit him flush on the nose. The main thing Charlie knew about fighting was that when it was time to swing, the one who hit first was usually the one who hit last.

The boy with the telephone dropped it, while the others muttered threateningly and moved around as if to jump in.

"Don't hurt anybody unless they mess in this, Caesar," he said. "It's between me and Cowboy. Don't give 'em that bolo punch unless you have to."

"Sure, mahn," Caesar said tersely, keeping his fists belt high and shuffling around a little.

Cowboy got up, his eyes streaming and blood pouring from his nose. As Charlie weaved before him, Cowboy made a futile stab at his head. Charlie faked one at Cowboy's face, then belted him in the stomach.

Cowboy doubled over. He fell to his hands and knees, gagging. Charlie waited long enough to be sure he was not going to get up with a board in his hand. But it was clear that Cowboy would not get up at all without help.

"Anybody else?" Charlie said. "Then don't fool with anything here. And be sure and take that phone when you leave, because we don't want it around. Don't come back, either."

Cowboy was still moaning and gagging. Charlie walked to where he had left the coins, put them in a tin can, and started for the street.

Chapter 10

Five Dollars a Smash

Nine cents apiece was the going price for used brick, Uncle Baron reported that night. The fifteen cents Ellis had talked of was what you'd have to pay if you bought them. Still, each brick was worth nearly a dime. And wine bottles went for a cent and a half. The bounty on rats was two bits.

"And I got two dollars for that old steering wheel!" he said.

"Look what I found!" Charlie said. He brought the rusty can of treasure from his room and dumped it on the table.

"What you been doing, robbing coke machines?" Roscoe Matthews asked.

"No, only pay phones," Charlie said. He told them about the find, while Uncle Baron and his father dug through the discolored coins.

"Huh!" Uncle Baron said. "These coins might be worth something."

"To who?" asked Charlie's mother. "You or the telephone company?"

"Oh, I wouldn't steal those poh folks' money,

Sis," said Uncle Baron, deadpan. "I'll put nine seventy-five in a pay phone somewhere." He winked at Charlie.

"I was talking to Ed Ortiz, the man who owns the business we're buying," he told Charlie. Got him down twenty-five dollars. But he's got to have the money two weeks from today. Else he'll sell to somebody else."

Charlie felt a whiplash of panic. *Don't sell, Ortiz!* he prayed.

When it was time for Charlie's dad to go to work, Uncle Baron said he would drive him. Exhausted, Charlie went to bed. But he could not sleep. He chewed his lip in misery. When he thought of someone else walking off with Ortiz's whatever-it-was, he groaned. What was the mystery deal? He pictured it as a machine of some sort. Perhaps it made things one could sell. A doughnut machine? A gadget to stamp out other gadgets?

It could be anything. But already in his mind it had the weight and bulk of a machine. It practically had to be one. He fell asleep imagining himself packing shiny, heavy little products in crates.

Next day Uncle Baron rented a trailer at a U-Haul lot. They loaded it with bricks, and he drove off. Charlie attacked the wall again. The chisel clinked against mortar and brick, and Charlie's arms grew rosy with dust. Before noon the blue bus roared back up Seneca Street. Uncle Baron had seven dollars and fifty cents in his leather clasp purse. He also brought a dime-store account book, in which he asked Charlie to enter the transaction.

Caesar arrived, and the Charlie-and-Caesar salvage machine began to hum. It was fun—*click, clunk, scrape*—nine cents cash! *Click, clunk*—another nine cents. They would clean and stack a pile of bricks; then one boy would stand in the trailer while the other tossed up the bricks and the trailer man stacked them.

Buster came for an hour and dug out a few dozen bottles, then vanished.

Uncle Baron returned near dusk. "Guess what! One of them nickels was worth thirteen dollars! A couple of other coins was worth over two dollars apiece. There wasn't anything worth less'n a quarter. I sold the whole lot for thirty dollars!"

They added up the day's take, and split it. Caesar got nine dollars and forty cents. Charlie and his uncle kept twenty-eight dollars and ten cents, which they sealed in an envelope for Mr. Toia.

Since you could not find a telephone every day, the following days were a letdown.

Broken dime-store jewelry and a rusty Mickey Mouse watch gave Charlie his biggest thrills. Through the week he hacked at the wall. He dropped a few rats with snap shots. But the classic car parts Ellis had talked of remained hidden with the heroes of some deeper layer of civilization.

The wall shrank—bricks going out, a little money coming in. Charlie's skill at demolition was fast putting them out of business. On Thursday, Uncle Baron hauled away the last of the bricks.

On Friday afternoon, he and Caesar realized they were down to pure junk. They dug and sifted, then gave up.

"The show is over and the monkey's dead," said Charlie. At the truck, Uncle Baron was cleaning a Chrysler hub cap with a wire brush. "That's it," Charlie told him. "All we've found today is two buttons, a rusty pocketknife, and a moldy mop."

"Then it's time to rent one of them pint-sized tractors and skin the lot off clean like we promised. You fellas stay here while I take the trailer back and put in for a tractor tomorrow."

In a half hour he was back with a sad face.

"They want a fifty-dollar deposit on a tractor. Tried to leave the bus, but they say the tractor is worth more'n what the bus is."

Charlie snapped his fingers. "Breathing Man!"

"What about him?"

"He'll know somebody that'll do it cheap."

Breathing Man, dozing in the blue afternoon shade, was mummified in brown garments—collar turned up on his overcoat, GI cap pulled down, hands buried in his pockets.

"Hello, Breathing Man," Charlie said.

Breathing Man's eyes opened. Smiling, he said, "Hello, Charlie."

"How're you feeling?" Charlie asked.

"Fine. Jus' fine."

"This is my Uncle Baron Crawford. And my buddy Caesar Étienne."

They all shook Breathing Man's thin hand. It was as cold and dark as a bird's foot.

"Got a problem," Charlie said, and he explained things.

Without hesitation, Breathing Man said: "Talk to Ed Spencer. He's inside, shooting pool."

"What's he got?"

"Skip loader and truck. Cheap and good."

Uncle Baron went inside.

Closing his eyes, Breathing Man said: "Been thinking about you, Charlie. Still trying to make money?"

"Sure am—and running scared."

"There's this fella Ray Tharp. Supervisor for the Park Department. Very bright. Was telling me about ladybugs."

Charlie looked at Caesar. "Ladybugs?"

"Them little red bugs. Eats bugs on plants. Park Department buys millions of them. Use ladybugs instead of poisons sometimes."

Breathing Man's hands went up and painstakingly drew the muffler about his throat. By his standards, it was a chilly day. About eighty-five.

"Uh-huh, but we don't have any ladybugs," Charlie said.

"Ray says folks collects them in the foothills. In cold weather they buddy up like bees. Though it's still almost too warm, he says."

"How about that?" Caesar remarked.

Charlie could think of nothing intelligent to say to anything so preposterous, so he, too, said, "Yeah, how about that?"

Breathing Man's hand groped inside his coat. A paper crackled. He pulled out a folded sheet of ruled dime-store stationery.

"Got it all right here," he said.

They put their heads together and read the paper.

Charlie Matthews. We pay eight dollars a gallon for ladybugs if in good condition. Would suggest such places as Sierra Molina Canyon. The ladybugs gather in colonies and are easily collected on cold nights. If you manage to collect any, contact me at the number below. Good luck. Ray Tharp.

At that moment Uncle Baron emerged, nodding happily. "Nice fellow. He'll clean the lot for seventy-five dollars."

"Wow," Charlie muttered.

But Uncle Baron said he thought they were still 'way ahead. "Let's look at the book, and see."

Charlie and Caesar sat in the bus and reckoned everything up:

Bricks, $126.00.
Rats, $ 5.50.
Coins, $ 30.00.
Bottles, .78.

This made a total of $162.28—more than enough for the investment. But hauling would knock that down to $87.28. Bad news. Charlie put his elbows on the table and parked his head in his hands.

"Breathing Man was talking about ladybugs," he told Uncle Baron, finally. "Guy that works for the Park Department will buy them from us."

"Let's take a crack at it," said Uncle Baron. "We only got another week to get up the money for Ortiz. This is Friday night. We'll take the chillun along and camp out tomorrow night."

"On the way," Charlie said, "we can stop and sell a pint of blood apiece. Breathing Man says they pay five dollars a smash."

Chapter 11

Ladybug, Ladybug!

Charlie's mother fixed sack lunches. Uncle Baron talked a bakery out of some flour sacks in which to carry the ladybugs. With Buster and Callie sitting in back, they left Dogtown.

On the way, they stopped at the blood bank. Uncle Baron, Charlie, and Caesar each lay on a table and sold a pint of blood. Afterward the nurse gave each donor a paper cup of juice and a little packet of iron pills.

"This will help you to grow more blood," she said brightly.

"Jus' like fertilizer on a crop," said Uncle Baron.

Charlie felt no different after the blood was withdrawn than before. He offered to sell another pint, but the nurse called a doctor, who explained how, if you gave too much blood, you would go into shock and possibly die. He decided to wait a few days.

Freeways carried them quickly across the city. From Dogtown they passed through a belt of small factories, then skimmed over thousands of tiny houses with little yards, each identical except for the colors of the roofs. The last freeway ended, and they squeezed into a two-lane highway choked with fast traffic. Trucks boomed past, rocking the bus with windy backwash. It was orange- and olive-grove country. Subdivisions were tucked in here and there. The kids gazed out in wonder.

"Don't reckon I've ever been so far from home before," said Callie timidly.

"Home is where your folks is at," said Uncle Baron, "and this bus is full of your folks. We'll stop soon and have lunch."

He pulled over at the next roadside rest. There were a stone drinking fountain, picnic benches, and a large tree. Charlie had brought a baseball, and they had a game of catch. Uncle Baron started the car again, and they piled in.

A few miles farther along, they turned toward a blue range of mountains. Below the mountains were rough brown foothills.

" 'Cording to the map, Sierra Molina Canyon's in them foothills," said Uncle Baron.

Towns were strung like beads on the narrow cement road. It was an old one, cracked like a plate and mended with tar. The towns all looked the same—compact little cores of buildings that loosened quickly into dry fields and infrequent farmhouses. They stopped in one village and had root-beer floats at a drive-in. It reminded Charlie dimly of southern towns—a gas station, a mama-and-papa grocery store, a few sheds. The other customers, all white, gazed at them curiously.

"I ain't seen any Negro people lately," Callie said.

"No, baby," chuckled her uncle, "but you're going to see a lot of ladybugs soon, and that's where the money is."

Soon the cement road gave out. On an unpaved country road they wandered along the edge of an immense dry wash a mile wide. Uncle Baron said that this was Sierra Molina Canyon and that they were in the heart of the ladybug country. Small side canyons choked with dusty live oak trees and brush emptied into the main canyon.

"I bet the Indians massacred lots of settlers here," Buster said eagerly. He uttered a war whoop that made Callie cry out angrily:

"Oh, shut up, Buster!"

Uncle Baron laughed. "No, no, this ain't massacre country," he said. "It's gold-rush country. Ain't you never heard of the Oak of the Golden Dream?"

Buster and Callie clutched the back of the front seat, anxious to hear about it.

Well, he told them, about a hundred years ago, a Mexican sheepherder had fallen asleep here under an oak tree. He dreamed that an angel told him to dig under the tree, and when he sank his knife in the earth it came up all crusty with gold nuggets!

But when he woke up, the earth was covered with dry oak leaves instead of gold nuggets. He was disgusted and hungry, and, not having brought lunch along, he pulled up a wild onion.

And by gollies, if there weren't hundreds of tiny flakes of gold caught in its roots!

Before the excitement was over, Uncle Baron said, thousands of men were digging for gold in this canyon. But the poor sheepherder had nothing much left but onions.

"And that's why I never mess around with gold rushes," he said. "I play it safe. You never heard of a ladybug rush, did you?"

The afternoon was wearing away. The air had a nip. They poked along, watching for a suitable campsite. The ravines were bone dry, but Uncle Baron had brought plastic jugs of water. The road was now more of a trail, but the bus lunged up and over the rocks and ruts. Charlie thought of camping out on the way across the country. He could hardly believe that his life was to be given such a spin.

The car slowed. To the right of the road lay a clear area among the oak trees. Brush and boulders outlined a perfect campsite.

"This must be the place!" said Uncle Baron.

Stiff with the long ride, they jumped out and ran around, posing on boulders like Napoleon, hurling rocks and broken branches.

Soon Uncle Baron said, "Now we get to work."

They cleared enough room for three people to sleep. Buster and Callie would sleep in the bus, the menfolk on a tarp spread on leaves. A cold dusk closed in as they finished making beds. Charlie and Caesar arranged rocks for a campfire, while Uncle Baron opened cans of beans and put wieners to boil.

Suddenly Buster came shrieking in. "Bugs!" he yelled. "Millions of 'em!"

"Where? What kind of bugs?" Charlie asked him.

Yelling unintelligibly, Buster ran up the road with everyone straggling after him, then took off up a rocky ravine. Down the middle of it ran a river of sand that flowed around the boulders. The brush was brittle, and smelled curiously like molasses and medicine. Some shrubs had tiny orange berries on the branches; some looked like holly; but most of them seemed meant primarily to puncture the hides of people crawling through.

"There! Lookit!"

Standing in the sand, Buster pointed at a shrub overhanging the ravine. Its branches appeared to be loaded with berries. But when Charlie looked more closely, he saw that they were ladybugs—thousands of them clustered together along the twigs and branches!

They crowded close to stare at the insect colony. Each ladybug, only an eighth of an inch across, was like a miniature turtle with a shiny red back. Callie crooned softly to them, her lips nearly touching the little red insects:

" 'Ladybug, ladybug, fly away home!
Your house is on fire, and—' "

"Don't say it!" said her uncle. "Land sakes, you want 'em to take off?" He chuckled.

"Listen!" she whispered. "You can hear 'em!"

Sure enough, the mass of insects gave off a muted rattling sound, like a million tiny shields clashing at a distance. Yet the bugs scarcely seemed to stir. They were simply hived up here, it seemed, to sleep.

"Ain't they a sight?" Uncle Baron marveled. "You know, I thought all along they was kidding us. But I figured we might as well have a little camping trip out of it. Charlie, lad, get the sacks—"

Two of them held a flour sack open under a branch, while the others shook it gently until clots of squirming red insects tumbled inside. A third of a sack was a pretty good load. Besides, Uncle Baron was afraid that too many in one sack would cause the bugs to go out of their minds or something.

Right up until dark they collected, working at last by flashlight. They hunted for more bug colonies, but found only a few small clusters. Finally, with two sacks partially filled, they trudged back to camp.

And now came the good time. They built the campfire and devoured wieners and beans, then sat on boulders around the fire. Callie stuck close to Uncle Baron, distrustful of the dark. Finished with eating, he got out his guitar and played the old songs he knew.

At last it was bedtime. Charlie felt as though he had been blessed. He lay under his blankets on the crackling leaves between Caesar and Uncle Baron, smiling at the stars, too full of joy to speak. Starting in a week or two, this was his life. He and Uncle Baron. Camping, driving, hoping, working.

Chapter 12

Fly Away Home!

The sun woke them early, bursting in glory over the mountains behind the canyon. They ate breakfast, then they spent an hour hunting more ladybug colonies. They realized at last how lucky they had been to find the one they did. All their searching turned up only a few more small clusters. Uncle Baron let them play for an hour. Then everything was loaded into the bus; the trash was burned in the fire ring, and the embers were doused with water. They headed back down Sierra Molina Canyon.

Back to Dogtown. Charlie wished they could drop the other kids off at a bus stop and keep right on rolling.

"Keeping them bugs out of the sun, ain't you?" Uncle Baron called back, once.

"Yes. No. One of 'em's—"

Sounds of Buster reaching back to move a sack. Then there was an ominous tearing sound.

Callie screamed, "Buster! You tore the sack!"

"I know! Help me!"

Charlie flung a startled look into the rear. Rusty smoke rose from the luggage space behind the kids. Smoke? No, he realized: it was a cloud of bugs!

The air was filled with winged red specks flying and settling. They made a humming sound. Uncle Baron slapped the back of his neck as one landed.

"Holy tomato!" he yelled. "What have you done?" He swerved the car to the side of the road.

Callie dragged the torn flour sack onto the seat between her and Buster. Charlie saw a foot-long rip in its side. The sack, so plump before, now sagged like the sides of a cat that had just had kittens. Callie tried to keep both hands over the tear, while Buster futilely scraped handfuls of ladybugs from the windows and attempted to stuff them into the sack.

But the insects kept whirling out. The windshield was nearly covered with them. Uncle Baron switched on the windshield wipers, then remembered that the bugs were on the wrong side of the glass. They clung to it; they fell; they swarmed up from the floor into their shoes and pants legs.

"Open the windows!" Callie screamed.

"No!" Charlie yelled back. "They'll get away!"

He saw the insects on his uncle's face, and tried to brush them off, but now they were crawling over his own face.

Buster reached for the doorlatch, but Uncle Baron shouted at him not to open it—the ladybugs would all fly out. They had to try, at least, to recover some of them.

Crawling in back with the others, Charlie managed to pull together the torn edges of the ripped sack. Bugs swarmed all over him—in his hair, his ears, his nostrils. He hefted the sack. There were still a few cupfuls in it.

"Gimme one of those other sacks!" he gasped.

"Where are they?" Callie cried.

"You put 'em in, I didn't!"

Callie found a sack beneath a seat. "Hold it open!" Charlie panted. "I'm gonna stuff this sack inside it."

With the torn sack inside a good one, he knotted the top of the sound one. Then he had Callie hold another sack open while they scooped ladybugs off the ceiling, the floor, the upholstery, and shook them into it. As soon as a handful was inside, she would hold the bag closed again.

It was a losing game. Thousands of insects swarmed over every surface. Half crazy with bugs inside their clothing, they gave up. But when they hurled the doors open, the ladybugs continued swarming pointlessly about in the bus.

"Okay, close the doors," sighed Uncle Baron. "We'll just have to drive home this way. After they cool off, they'll hive up again."

Everyone kept busy scraping and scooping. It was the sort of project a lifer might set himself in his cell to keep from going crazy. *Ladybug Man of Alcatraz,* Charlie thought, dropping a few more insects into a sack.

Because of the bugs on the windshield, Uncle Baron was forced to drive slowly. It was late afternoon before they reached Dogtown. He turned up the alley and eased into the yard. They all began stripping off shirts and running combs through their hair.

"Jus' leave everything be," Uncle Baron said. "We'll git after 'em again when it's cool."

Everyone wanted a bath, so by the time Charlie got a shot at the tub all the hot water was gone. Still, if felt good to get clean. Afterward, he went out to look at the bus. The little beetles were still swarming around.

He suggested that Uncle Baron call Ray Tharp and see when and where they could deliver the bugs. But Tharp did not answer. Saturday night: For all they knew, he might be gone for the weekend.

Uncle Baron had to sleep on the broken-down sofa. On Sunday morning, hearing him in the bathroom, Charlie dressed quickly. They went out together to see how the bugs were doing. Chilled, they had magically quieted down. With care, they scraped them from all the surfaces they could reach. Hundreds of dead beetles lay on the floor and seats. Charlie swept them out. It was plain that many days would pass before the last ladybug was smoked out.

Evening came before they reached Mr. Tharp. He told them to bring the bugs over to his house. In the morning he would take them to work and get what he could for them.

Chapter 13

The Nitty Gritty

Early the next morning Charlie trotted over to Leonard's to catch Mr. Toia on the way to school. Leonard's new boy had not shown up yet. Sometimes, Leonard told Charlie, he did not come until two or three o'clock.

"Ain't many fellows as steady as you," he said.

Charlie was telling him about the ladybug hunt when he heard the popping of the teacher's little motorcycle. He ran out to flag him down. Mr. Toia came in to hear the rest of the ladybug story. Afterward, he said, laughing, "Charlie, if you don't write that up for me, I'll sic the attendance worker on you."

Charlie was flattered. "I'll write it tonight," he said. Then: "Say, Mr. Toia. I'm going to need all my money Friday afternoon. Could you bring it here? I'd pick it up, but I may be on the principal's most-wanted list by now."

"I think you probably are. I'll bring it here after school."

"Thanks," Charlie said.

A few minutes after Mr. Toia had left, Ellis and Woodson, the slum lords, dropped in looking as curried and pink-skined as a couple of prize stockyard animals. When they climbed up on the chairs, Charlie got to work on Ellis's shoes. Ellis said they had checked the lot, and it looked fine.

"Did you make any money?" he asked.

"Nickels and dimes," Charlie said, grinning.

Woodson said: "I suppose you're so rich now that we'll never get you to put on a fight at one of our smokers, eh?"

Charlie worked smartly with the cloth, his mind weaving carefully through the ins and outs of the situation. It was quite possible that their ladybugs were all of the wrong kind—nearsighted, too many spots, or something. To scratch up the last few dollars, he might have to resort to something he would ordinarily turn his nose up at. So he said politely:

"I was talking to my buddy about it, but he isn't sure he wants to. Can I call you somewhere if he changes his mind?"

Woodson, somewhat grumpily, gave him a business card. "You can leave a message if I'm not there."

Sure enough, Ray Tharp called that night with bad news.

"All I could get for you was thirty-two dollars,"

he told Uncle Baron. "We had to crawl-clean the bugs before we weighed them, you see. The Department buys only the fast crawlers."

It figured, Charlie thought wearily. With all the lively bugs in the state, they had to bring home a gunny sack full of bums.

But Uncle Baron eagerly rubbed his hands together. "Get the book, Charlie. Let's tote this up."

Charlie got the account book, and Uncle Baron sat thrumming his guitar as he worked. Using everything but geometry, Charlie reckoned up who got how much and what the total was. His stomach iced up as he looked at the sum.

$121.28.

He dropped his hands in his lap. "It's not enough. We need another thirty dollars. Maybe we could get another bunch of ladybugs—"

"No. We really combed those canyons before we left. We got the last ladybug in the hills. Add it up again."

Charlie did. The figures were right.

"Pshaw," said Uncle Baron, laying the guitar aside.

Charlie went out to the bus and turned on the dome lights. New colonies of ladybugs had formed on the lights. He heard Uncle Baron come out. For a while they mumbled about ladybugs, but their minds were on other things.

"Wouldn't Ortiz trust us for the rest?" Charlie suggested.

"Him? When he was a baby," Uncle Baron said, "Ortiz wouldn't trust his mother for milk. He wanted milk tickets."

"If—if we don't get the money," Charlie said, "can't I come along anyway? I'll make money for you—"

Uncle Baron sighed. "Nothing I'd like better, Charlie. But I can't take a chance on getting stranded, and no money to feed my sister's boy. I guess I got too much whatyoucallit—responsibility."

"I *think* I can get the rest, then. But I can't get it before Friday night."

Uncle Baron dropped both hands on his shoulders and stared into his eyes. "Are you joshing me?"

Charlie shook his head. Uncle Baron squeezed his shoulders hard. "I never saw the like of you, all my born days! You're a scrapper. A real scrapper."

I'd better be, Charlie thought.

Early the next morning, like a man blowing on a pair of cold dice to warm them up, Charlie visited Breathing Man. He had no real hope that the old man could come up with a better idea than the fight, but it wouldn't cost anything to ask him.

He found him propped in his chair before Sam's Hob Nob, nibbling a coffeecake with small fierce bites like a squirrel. His thin fingers revolved the pastry. He paused often to tend to his breathing. His head turned when he saw Charlie, and he smiled.

"Hello, Charlie. Help yourself. To a coffeecake." Under his chair rested a greasy paper bag. Charlie thanked him and grubbed out a Danish pastry. They ate a while, buddy-fashion. Then Charlie explained his problem. Breathing Man pondered.

"Hmm. Well, well. Maybe you could get your teacher to help. Boy I knew once got second-rate candy. From a candy factory. Sold it door to door. Around Christmas time, it was. Teacher got it for him."

"It's a long way to Christmas," Charlie said. "That would be *little* bread, too. I need big bread."

Then he told about the fight.

"*That's* big bread!" said Breathing Man. "Why don't you fake it?"

"Fake it?"

"Like on TV. Grunt-and-groan rasslers. Cowboy fights."

"Hey, hey, hey!" Charlie said. "Just pretend to hit hard, huh?"

"There you go! Fake it."

"We'd have to practice. *Maybe* it would fool them. I wonder—"

"Get some blood. At a slaughterhouse. And some little balloons—"

Charlie smacked his fist into his palm. "That's it! When we get through fighting, they'll have to hose out the ring!"

After school he set out to find Caesar. He knew he lived in Osuna Village, a housing project near the freeway. But so did several thousand other people. However, a boy named Cool Hankins also lived there, and as Charlie roamed the curving streets with their ratty lawns and areaways glistening with broken glass, he saw Cool's huge old Buick gliding up, its nose scraping the blacktop like a hound sniffing a trail.

Charlie flagged him down.

"What's happening?" Cool asked. He was a good-looking boy who hung in with a crowd over near the Boys' Club.

"I'm looking for that West Indian kid, Caesar Something-or-Other."

"Ay-tin—Caesar Ay-tin. Climb in. I just seen him hanging out wash for his old lady. He lives near me. Wait'll I untie this here wire—"

The door was wired shut on the right side, in the absence of a latch. Cool made a U-turn, and they blue-smoked along through a jungle of flat-roofed buildings with bright stucco walls—yellow, green, pink, brown. Kids swarmed the streets and court-yards and dropped gravel from the rooftops on kids below. On the freeway, which soared along near the buildings, cars whooshed by and trucks droned and roared.

Cool stopped. "See that there pink building next to the green one? In between there's a courtyard. I seen him carrying wash in there. That kid's square enough to fit in a shoebox. Whattayou want him for?"

"He's my buddy. He's okay."

"Oh. Excuse it, man."

A couple of Mexican ladies were hanging out laundry and screeching at their kids in two languages. Among these small plump women and pygmy-sized children stood Caesar, six-feet-five, hanging up wash.

Charlie thought: *A kid that'll hang up laundry will do anything for money. I'm in.*

With a mouthful of clothespins, Charlie helped him for a while.

"What's going on?" Caesar asked, finally.

Charlie told him. At first all Caesar could do was to scowl. But as Charlie explained, he began to smile.

Charlie said: "And we each got a little plastic tube, like a hair-goop tube, in each hand, see? Every now and then we squeeze one. There'll be blood all over the place! Those finks will be out of their minds."

"I don't think they have any minds, but they'll be out seventy-five dollars. Okay by me, Charlie."

Chapter 14

The Brawl

That night Charlie telephoned Mr. Woodson and said that he and Caesar would put on the fight. Woodson said: "Great! I'll put you on my Friday night card. Pick you up at the shine parlor at seven o'clock. Wear gym trunks under your clothes."

After dinner Charlie took Uncle Baron outside. "I'll have another thirty-seven-fifty Friday night," he said. "So tell Ortiz to have the machine ready."

"The machine—?" Uncle Baron stroked his chin with his fingertips.

"I mean—whatever it is."

"Oh, yes—the investment. 'Machine' isn't far off, at that. It's a thing that does a job for you, and then you collect the money. That kind of a machine." Then he put his hand on Charlie's shoulder. "Charlie-boy, it's not drugs or anything, is it? You're not going to carry horse for some peddler, are you?"

"Ain't I got headaches enough without that? It's not drugs, nossir."

"Okay, then. I'll drive over tonight when you bring the money, and talk to Ortiz."

Charlie searched the house for containers suitable for blood, but everything was too large. The thing needed to be about the size of a roll of dimes, capable of being hidden in a clenched fist. He decided to look in the dime store tomorrow. They would have to get over to a slaughterhouse sometime Friday, too.

Already, somewhere in his gizzard, a little nerve quivered like the hairspring of a watch. And a thought fretted him that a man smart enough to drive a gunmetal Cadillac might be too smart to be fooled by animal blood when he was paying for fresh human blood.

The rest of the week, Uncle Baron cleaned the car. He had his own greasing tools, and jacked the bus up and lubed it. Clearly, he was on the wing. From a closet in the bus, he dug out a red and white-striped tent affair and rigged it up beside the bus. He produced a neat folding cot and an old sleeping bag, and told Charlie the tent would be his bedroom.

Charlie almost bawled.

Friday afternoon.

Charlie settled on some clear plastic squeeze tubes from the dime store. They were filled with a hair cream called *On Top*. He squeezed out the goop, refilled them with water, and punctured each tube with a pin. When he squeezed them, they squirted a thin stream of water.

Uncle Baron tracked down a slaughterhouse and brought home a bottle of animal blood. Charlie had finally told him what the blood was for. Uncle Baron thought it was a good joke, but he warned:

"You kids be careful, now. You don't need any front teeth broken."

After school, Mr. Toia brought the money in an envelope. In the envelope were a listing of all Charlie's deposits, and an extra dollar he said was interest. He tried to talk to Charlie about education, and staying with it, and not settling for a fast buck when the slow buck was more likely to stick to your fingers. Charlie said that he understood. Mr. Toia offered his hand.

"If I don't see you again, Charlie," he said, "I wish you the best of luck. Write me a letter soon."

"I sure will, Mr. Toia." Charlie wanted to say more about appreciating the teacher's interest in him and all, but he was embarrassed to put it in words. He decided he would write him a nice letter and tell him these things. It was always easier to write a thing than to say it, he thought.

All Charlie could stomach for dinner was a little chocolate milk and coffee. His heart pounded and he felt dry-mouthed and feverish. In a mildewed flight bag he had brought home from the lot, he stored four squeeze bottles of blood, a tube of Vaseline, and a towel. Vaseline smeared on the face kept you from cutting so easily, he had heard. If anybody got onto the blood trick, he might be required to do some bleeding himself.

At six thirty he jogged over to the shine stand. Leonard's supplies were locked under a hinged cover. He smelled meat frying in Leonard's living quarters in the rear. Leonard invited Charlie in, and they talked until Caesar showed up. The West Indian boy was nervous, too. He kept chewing his lip and picking up things on the table and putting them down.

"You fellas are as jumpy as though you were getting married," Leonard said. "Take it easy."

An auto horn blared. The boys jumped.

"Listen," Charlie said hastily, "if they catch on, we'll have to swing a few. But after a couple of rounds I'll take a dive. If you haven't already kayoed me."

"Well, I think that's what they want—just a couple of Christians for the lions to tear up. But we'll have to act like lions, too—some of the time—"

Woodson swung the car door open as they trudged from the shine parlor. "We can all ride in front." He was grinning.

They took off. Woodson got on the freeway, then looked at them, and chuckled. "Relax," he told them. "This isn't a real brawl you're going to put on.

You'll be fighting under special rules that'll make it easier on you."

"What kind of rules?" Charlie asked, suspicious.

Woodson laughed. "Just rules."

"Where's it gonna be?"

"Ever heard of the Balboa Hippodrome?"

"Uh-huh. Downtown?"

"That's right."

Charlie shifted uneasily. "Well, that's a real boxing club, isn't it?"

"You bet it is. And I'm a real promoter."

"Well, see, Caesar and I aren't real boxers, Mr. Woodson, so—"

Woodson patted his knee. "That's why I wanted you, Charlie. After the regular matches, you and Caesar are going to give them some laughs. It'll be fun for everybody."

Well, almost everybody, Charlie thought.

Woodson swung the Cadillac down an offramp into a downtown area. The buildings were all old and dingy. He slowed at an intersection. On one corner, Charlie saw a large brick church, on another, a gas station, and next to the gas station a two-story wooden structure that occupied a full half-block. A neon sign on the roof glowed in the night.

BALBOA HIPPODROME

As Woodson parked in front, a young man standing near the box office hurried to the curb. Woodson stepped out, but told the boys to stay in the car.

"How's the gate?" he asked the man, who wore a uniform with BALBOA HIPPODROME stitched on the back.

"Pretty good, Mr. Woodson."

"Take these boys around to the side entrance. Show them to the dressing room after you park the car."

Charlie began questioning the attendant as soon as he drove into the alley beside the building. "What do we have to do? We aren't really boxers, man—"

The man smiled. "You'll fight with gloves as big as pillows, and just kind of mash each other around. You'll have as much fun as anybody, and if you really put on a good show, they'll throw money at you. Nothing to it."

He led them through a side door of the barny old building into a dimly-lit hall that smelled like a vacuum cleaner bag full of stale popcorn. The wooden walls, ceiling and floor looked so dry that Charlie figured if you dropped a match the whole works would go off like a firecracker. Evidently the Fire Department thought so, too, because there was a fire extinguisher every few yards and *Exit* signs and arrows at every turn.

They came to an open door and the attendant walked inside. Charlie stepped timidly after him into a large room with battered metal lockers lining the walls. There were a toilet in an alcove, a number of benches where men in boxing trunks and robes sat or lay resting, some scales, and a washbowl. Bolted to the wall was a metal box with a red cross on it and the words, *First Aid.*

"Take a locker and make yourselves comfortable," said the attendant. "Mr. Woodson will tell you when you go on."

The boys stripped to their gym clothes. No one paid any attention to them. In the bowels of the hippodrome, an organ was playing the national anthem; there was a muted thunder of people standing up and singing. A man thrust his head in the door.

"Lopez and Mills, let's *go!*"

Two men in dressing robes went out.

Charlie and Caesar sat biting their lips and listening to occasional fits of shouting from the arena. Most of the fighters showed signs of nervousnesss. One of them, a white man about twenty-five whose arms were covered with tattooing, chewed on a stub of a cigar and skipped rope.

Lopez and Mills returned, blood on the Mexican's face, a skinned place on Mills' brow. Both men were breathing hard. Two others went out, flexing their arms. A rank odor of perspiration, stronger than any smell Charlie remembered, filled the room. If came from the men who had been fighting, and it turned his stomach. They went into the showers.

This is like the stockyards or something, Charlie thought, in a vague panic.

He weighed himself, scratched, lay down, sat up, and frowned at his feet. Caesar muttered, "Cool, man. It's only blood."

Three fights were run off, the contestants coming back winded and battered each time, one man sniffing smelling salts that a man in shirtsleeves —possibly his manager—held under his nose.

Then two light heavyweights went out. Just after the fight started there was a burst of shouting, a vocal explosion that shook the windows. After that there was some applause; then a strange silence. The boxers in the locker room looked at one another. Finally one of the light heavies returned.

"Jeez, he went down like—" he gestured. "Hell, I hardly laid a glove on him." He looked around for sympathy. "I guess he hit his head or something."

The injured fighter was carried in on a stretcher, finally. A doctor worked over him. The man had a bruise on his chin, but no blood showed. He was white as marble. Woodson sauntered in and stood by.

"Shall I call the wagon?" he asked.

"Yes. It's a concussion."

After they carried out the unconscious man, Charlie clutched at Woodson's arm. "Look, we changed our—"

Woodson shoved at him some big boxing gloves from a carton. "Here—put these on! You couldn't hurt each other if you tried. Take your shoes off first—you'll fight barefoot. All you're going to do is give the crowd some laughs. I was saving you till after the main event, but I think I'll use you now to get their minds off that last bout. Nobody's going to get hurt. Relax."

"Well, if—"

"Attaboy!" Woodson said.

Charlie took the Vaseline from his bag and smeared it on his face. Then he slipped the plastic tubes out and he and Caesar stored them under their armpits.

Chapter 15

"Come Out Fighting"

Some workmen were stretching a sheet of clear plastic over the mat when Woodson led the boys up through a trapdoor below the ring. The organ was booming out a lighthearted tune. The audience, visible through rocking layers of smoke and dust, seemed subdued. Charlie watched, puzzled, as workmen poured bottles of mineral oil on the plastic. In large shiny puddles it spread slowly over the mat.

"What's the idea of the goop?" he asked Woodson.

"That's to keep you from getting hurt. You'll slide with the punches, see?" Woodson said.

Suddenly one of Charlie's tubes of blood fell to the mat. He groaned. Woodson picked it up. "What's this?" He squeezed it and a big drop of animal blood formed on the tip. Suddenly he began to chuckle. "Fabulous! Has your buddy got one too?"

Puzzled but relieved, Charlie grinned and nodded.

"Great! Great! They'll catch on, but they'll love it anyway."

The ring announcer pulled down a microphone on a cord. "Brought to you at great expense," his words rang from a battery of loudspeakers, "are a pair of battlers from Outer Burbank. Charlie Matthews in the gray trunks, Caesar Ay-tin in the red. Six rounds of boxing under strict back alley rules. Come out fighting, and may the best man win!"

The bell rang. Someone jabbed Charlie with a thumb.

He decided, as he started across the ring, that they might as well earn their money. Nobody was going to get hurt with gloves big enough to put a baby to sleep on. He rushed out to meet Caesar. They collided in a pool of oil, skidded wildly, swung, and went flat on their backs.

Shining with oil, they got up. Charlie was excited and slightly dizzy. For a moment he and Caesar skidded around trying to get set. They swung. Both fell flat again. It hurt Charlie this time. He heard the crowd begin to laugh. The organ did some bumps-and-grinds music.

He got up slowly, to walk into a roundhouse blow to the top of his head. Down he went again. As he lay there, dazed, he saw the room through a bloody film. Panicky, he pawed blood from his eye. Then he realized he had accidentally squeezed blood in his own eye.

Carefully he stood up, measured as Caesar circled him, swung, and lost his balance. Caesar got busy recovering his own balance. They sparred around. There was blood all over Caesar's chest and face.

"Who's cut? Who's cut?" a man yelled.

The boys grinned at each other. They were getting the hang of it; squirt a little blood as you punched, fall down, get up again. For a moment they windmilled viciously without striking a blow.

The bell rang. Charlie's arms were leaden with a fiery muscular ache.

Sitting on the stool, he gasped for breath. Woodson, in his corner, fanned him with a towel. Another man was tending Caesar. "Save yourself," Woodson told Charlie. "Let him do the swinging for a while, then plaster him when he slows down."

Charlie nodded. The bell clattered again; wearily he pushed himself up. The organist started on some slow, tired music that grew more brisk as the fighters moved faster. Every time anyone went down, there was a long, diminishing whistle and a crash of cymbals.

The boys skidded and bled for two more rounds before anyone got hurt. Then it was Charlie. He took one on the mouth, felt his lip ballooning, and spat out some real blood. He was smeared up now like an accident victim. The bell clanged and he sat panting on his stool. His vision was blurred with oil, but he saw coins landing around his feet. Though he needed rest, money was the name of the game. He slid off the stool and began collecting coins. The crowd laughed, and a few wadded bills fluttered down. He grabbed for them as the crowd cheered. Other bills and coins landed.

Woodson gave Charlie a shove as the bell rang. Staggering, the boys clinched and tried to rest. The organ played *Waltzing Matilda*. Exhausted, they squared off again and threw a few heavy-armed blows. Charlie missed with one and landed on his face. He was fairly sure they had fought at least twenty rounds when Woodson tossed a towel at him as he staggered back after the bell.

"That's it!" the promoter said.

More money sprinkled the mat. For a couple of minutes Charlie and Caesar crawled around picking it up. The announcer pulled down the mike.

"The fight is declared a draw!"

In the dressing room, Woodson counted out thirty-seven-fifty to each boy. They showered, dressed, and during the main event divided up their mat-winnings. Sixty-two dollars apiece, total!

Charlie figured. He needed only thirty more to bring the investment up to a hundred and fifty, which left him with thirty-two for himself. He had never been so tired nor so happy.

Very late, Woodson dropped him before his

house. Sleepy, sore and dazed, Charlie staggered up the walk. The excitement in his blood had burned out. Uncle Baron, waiting up, counted the money again while he took a bath. Charlie's father was at work and his mother was asleep.

Uncle Baron came to the bathroom and opened the door a few inches. "Charlie-boy, you really done it!" he said. "I got to get over to Ortiz's place, now. He's waiting up for me. I'll see you in the morning."

Chapter 16

Captain Teach

All night Charlie tossed. Bruised and feverish, his jaw aching, he kept waking with a pain mashed up under the top of his skull like a strawberry. Once he dreamed he heard a rooster crowing. There were no chickens in Dogtown, and it made him think of the farm in Georgia when he was very small.

At last it was daylight. Overhead, Buster's bottom still shaped the bedsprings. Charlie lay there incapable of anything but breathing. How much of it had he dreamed? Grease, blood, and dancing girls. Those Patriots had wild ideas about entertainment.

Someone tapped at the bedroom door. He smelled a cigar. Uncle Baron entered and smiled at Charlie.

"You 'wake?"

"Uh-huh."

"Better get up. You'll have to pack, 'cause we want to take off about noon."

Excitement seized Charlie like a cyclone, whirling him about. The machine!

"Did you get it?" he asked, sitting up.

Uncle Baron neatly knocked ash from his cigar into a pants cuff. "You better believe I got it," he said. "It's in the bus."

Charlie leaped to the floor. "No, no—take your time. Wash up and have your breakfast; then I'll show it to you."

It was Saturday; everyone was still asleep. Charlie ate cereal, while Uncle Baron drank a cup of coffee, smiling fatly and puffing his cigar.

Charlie gulped down a mouthful. "How much you reckon we'll make with it today?"

"Hard to say. Three hundred wouldn't be far off."

"Three hundred dollars!" Charlie dropped the spoon.

"Now, you understand we won't do that *every* day. But on the days we work, and depending on where we're at, we'll take in from fifty to three hundred bucks."

"What is it?" Charlie begged.

"If you ever get through stuffin' yourself, I'll show you." Uncle Baron laughed.

Charlie scrambled up. "I'm finished!"

Uncle Baron led the way to the back yard. Opening the side door of the bus, he paused to brush a little colony of ladybugs from the stove. From the curtained interior came a prolonged, brassy cry. It sounded to Charlie like a rooster crowing, and he remembered dreaming of chickens.

"Shut up, idiot," chuckled Uncle Baron. "You'll get yourself arrested."

Puzzled, Charlie trailed him into the bus. Something there *smelled* like a chicken, too. Uncle Baron closed the door and turned on the lights. He had made his bed and folded it away, so that it was once again a seat. On the seat rested a chicken-wire cage about two feet square. Within it stood a powerful greenish-black rooster with a golden eye set in a small black head.

"There's our little beauty!" said Uncle Baron. "His name is Captain Teach."

Charlie put a hand on the stove. He looked around for a machine. He saw nothing new but the rooster.

"A chicken?" he croaked. "A hundred and fifty bucks for a *chicken*?"

"That's no chicken, boy. That there is a fighting cock—murder and mayhem in feathers. That is the proud son of three hundred years of birds that lived for nothing but to kill. And he's all ours."

Charlie's head hummed. His brains had been given a whirl. "A hundred and fifty bucks?"

Uncle Baron twisted the cigar back and forth in his teeth, smiling.

"A bird ain't worth a cent more'n what you earn by betting on him. Captain Teach cost us seventy-five bucks. The other seventy-five is ours—for bets.

We're pitting him in Del Cerro Hills this afternoon."

"Isn't cockfighting against the law?" Charlie asked feebly.

"Well, technically. That's why the fights are held up this little canyon, see? Well, what do you think?"

What Charlie thought was that Caesar must have hit him too hard last night, because obviously someone in this bus was crazy.

"I—gee, I don't know. Don't know much about fighting cocks."

"That's all right. Your old uncle knows all there is to know about them. I've been pitting birds for twenty-some years. Down South and around Mexican tracks there's a fight 'most every weekend. Another thing—this bird is going to be the pappy of a lot of other fighters, and we'll get ten or fifteen dollars for his services, just like with a stud horse. Oh, we'll make us a hatful with him! This is the finest bird I've ever owned, bar none. And, Charlie-boy, I'm much obliged to you for all your help. We're pardners now. Ain't that so?"

Charlie, in a faint voice, said it was so.

Uncle Baron took the bird from the cage, tucked its head under his arm, and held its tail forward for Charlie to stroke. The feathers were stiff and glossy. The rooster's feet and legs were big and powerful. Its body was small, and it had been bred for one purpose alone; to fight.

"How do they fight?" Charlie asked. "Just chase each other around in the brush?"

"They fight in a little ring, like boxers—a pit, they call it. And you put little knives on their spurs, and they use them on each other like daggers. I'll teach you all about it. Right now I've got to mix up some enlivener to help him when he's fighting."

"What's enlivener?"

"That's my secret. It starts with whiskey and ends with red pepper, and there's thirteen other ingredients in between. Now, then, here's what we're gonna do. Pack everything you want to take. We'll leave it here and go over to the fights. Afterward we'll come back for supper, and then take off. How's that?"

Charlie said it was great. He ran into the house to start packing. He felt as he had last night after Woodson poured the vodka into him: Excited on the surface, scared and sick underneath. He knew that if the other bird were wearing knives, too, Captain Teach might be the one to get killed. And if he did, it was a hundred and fifty dollars down the tubes.

Yet even that was not important. What was important was that, win or lose, he had bought in with Uncle Baron. They were partners now. This was his last day in Dogtown.

Chapter 17

Shakebag

Uncle Baron said he had driven over to Del Cerro Hills with Ed Ortiz last night when he picked up the bird, so he knew the way. Gliding from freeway to freeway like a bubble in a blood vessel, the bus wormed its way from Dogtown. It crossed the middle of the big city, then swerved southeast.

Looking down on acres of tiny houses set among palm and pepper trees, Charlie recognized the area known as The Hole. Beyond The Hole were lumpy gray hills almost bare of trees, but with gray brush and live oaks filling the creases where hills met or had been gouged out by rain. Already the rains of autumn had worked a subtle undercolor of green into the dead grass. Here and there he could see a little colony of spidery oil derricks behind chain-link fencing.

The bus headed toward the foothills. They left the last of the ramshackle houses and headed up a little canyon much like Sierra Molina was, but smaller and with only a few starved-looking oaks along the road.

A Mexican sitting on a boulder beside the road got up and waved them to a stop. He came around and said to Uncle Baron:

"This is private property, mister. You'll have to go back."

"Ortiz sent me," Uncle Baron said.

The man grinned. "*Pásele,*" he said. "Good luck, eh?"

They drove on. Just beyond a turn they came into a clearing like a picnic ground. Many cars were parked among the oaks. Green winter grass an inch high made the ground like a carpet. Even before Uncle Baron stopped the engine, Charlie heard the crowing of roosters. Captain Teach heard it and began a lusty crowing.

Charlie gazed over the scene. At a counter made of plywood laid across two crates, a man was selling beer from a washtub filled with ice. Near the trees stood a long shelter of poles supporting a roof thatched with dry palm fronds. Beneath it was a little ring about twenty feet across, made of canvas tacked to two-foot stakes. Among the trees were many cages similar to Captain Teach's. Men strolled around chatting; many of them carried roosters, the heads buried under the owners' arms.

Charlie stuck close to his uncle. As far as he could see, there was no plan to the drifting and talking. Interest in these beautiful fighting birds made everyone a member of a club. The talk was of reds, grays, and spangles. Men praised Captain Teach, and compared him to someone else's "stag" or "blinker." A man said Ed Ortiz had bought a beautiful Irish dark-red this morning.

"Gonna be a pity to send Ed home with a pan-fryer," said Uncle Baron, "but he should've known better than to sell Captain Teach. What weight is his new bird?"

"Shakebag," the man said. "Ortiz can't hardly handle him."

"A man-fighter won't fight another bird, either," said Uncle Baron. "Maybe Ed don't know that."

The man examined Captain Teach closely, and drifted on.

Charlie began to realize the purpose of the socializing. The men were sizing up the birds and deciding how to bet.

A young Mexican carrying a brick-red bird under his arm approached them. Uncle Baron said it was Ortiz. Charlie watched the men shake hands. Ortiz was like a fighting cock himself, tall, well built, and with the dignity of a young tiger. He wore suntan pants and a white shirt with short sleeves.

"Whattayou got there, Ed?" asked Uncle Baron. "Ain't that a mother hen?"

Ortiz squatted and set the bird on the ground. It was a tough-looking gamebird with a grotesquely small body balanced on stout legs and feet. Charlie saw a powerful neck under bronze hackles. The cock suddenly seized a pinch of Ortiz's hand in its bill. Ortiz chuckled.

"That's a *bird, compadre,"* he said.

"Will he fight birds as good as he fights you?" asked Uncle Baron.

"I bought him from a catalogue, so I don't really know," the young Mexican said. "But I'm putting some money on him."

"How much?"

"Fifty dollars."

"He goes shakebag?"

Ortiz nodded, and Uncle Baron stroked his bird and said, "Well, I reckon my man could make the weight."

"You'd have to cut off a leg to fight him any lighter."

Charlie's head swam. A few days ago he had been cleaning bricks for nine cents apiece. Now Uncle Baron was betting fifty dollars on a rooster.

The crowd around the pit grew denser. Two men with watches stood in the ring. Other men with fighting birds roamed about, displaying the battlers. A man shouted something in Spanish, and all but two men holding fighting cocks got out of the pit.

Uncle Baron knelt and pulled a bottle from his hip pocket. "Hold the bird for me," he told Charlie. "Keep your hands open and flat."

Pressing his palms against the small body, Charlie was surprised to find how hard and heavy it was. He kept Captain Teach's wings tight against his body while Uncle Baron pried his bill open with one hand and poured a few drops of his secret enlivener down his throat. The bird made a squawk and shook its head.

"When does he fight?" Charlie asked.

"Later. The lightest birds go first. He'll be one of the last. The last fight of all will be a battle royal—all the cripples and broken-bills and the like will fight to the last man for a purse. You can go over and watch the action while I take care of him."

Charlie squeezed up near the pit and watched preparations for the first fight. Most of the conversation was in Spanish. The two men who held the birds walked around displaying them while bets were made. The referee stepped into the pit and made a line in the dirt. Then he made a parallel line about two feet away on each side of it.

"Come to the scores!" he called.

The handlers brought their birds to the lines in the earth. One of the birds was a dark red, the other a spangled green.

"Bill them," ordered the referee.

The handlers moved forward. Still holding the cocks, they let them peck at each other's heads with a hollow clacking of bills. Each bird wore a little knife about an inch long on his heels; the curved knives were covered with a plastic sheath.

"Ready!" called the referee.

The plastic sheaths were drawn; the birds were set on the ground. Seeing the razor-sharp little knives and the sudden ferocious straining of the birds, Charlie felt his heart pound with excitement. The birds thrust their heads out, neck hackles rising in a feathering ring; the small, almost combless heads in the center of the feathers were like the center of a target.

"Pit your birds!"

The birds flew together, rising several feet in the air as they struck with their bills. Then they fell back and circled each other, raising and lowering their heads. The green bird flew at the red, and the red flapped up to meet him. Feathers flew.

"*Pluma! Pluma!*" a man cried.

As far as Charlie could tell, not being a rooster, the idea seemed to be to get as high as possible above the other bird in order to be able to sink in the gaffs. The green bird now flew a split second before the red, and spurred down at his head. He missed the head and the gaff went into the wing feathers. They fell and struggled in the earth.

"Hung bird! Handle your birds!" the referee ordered.

The man who owned the gaffed bird squatted and

carefully removed the spur from the wing where it was fast. Blood sprinkled the ground and the feathers. The handlers worked on the fighters. The owner of the red bird blew in his bill, then took half the bird's head in his mouth for a moment to warm the comb. The other man blew on a spot near his fighter's tail.

"*Time*!" the referee called.

The birds fought until both were too tired to rise. Again they were handled and revived, and again they were pitted. After several more rounds, the exhausted gladiators lay with their heads together but unable to move. A man counted. Though Charlie did not understand why, the green bird was declared the winner.

In the crowd, money changed hands.

Charlie watched four more fights. One bird was blinded in an eye, but still won the fight. Another took a brain blow and sank down paralyzed. Some of the things the handlers did to injured birds turned his stomach. A hot match was used to close a cut blood vessel on a big gray bird's neck. Another was treated for a broken leg by simply removing the gaff on the bad leg; then it was sent back to fight until it died. A bird with a broken wing had its wing feathers hastily clipped off and returned to combat with the broken wing dragging.

"Shakebags next," the referee called.

"That's us!" Uncle Baron said.

Charlie had a sunk feeling. Entrusting a hundred and fifty dollars to a bird with a brain the size of a pea did not make sense to him. But it was too late to back out now.

Chapter 18

"Catch the R Bus"

Uncle Baron puffed nervously on his cigar. Charlie followed him through the crowd to where he had tied Captain Teach by one leg to a tree. The afternoon was wearing out in coolness and long shadows. Kneeling, Uncle Baron laid out strips of old glove leather, waxed thread, and sheathed gaffs.

"Hold him while I heel him," he said. He showed Charlie how he wanted the bird held.

Charlie held the hard little body while his uncle wrapped the cock's ankle with leather, then fitted the razorlike spurs in place and tied them with thread. He tested their tightness, then stood up.

Holding Captain Teach with his head under his arm, he strolled back to where the timekeeper sat on the bumper of a car near the pit. Charlie stayed close to him. Scared and excited, he kept trying to moisten his lips with a tongue as dry as flannel. He wished it were over and they were on the road. He could see where Captain Teach might be a fine investment, but he could also see him being carried out with his head hanging and blood running from his bill.

More yelling broke out as a fight was finished. A man came through carrying a dead bird, a beautiful Dominique with a rose-colored comb and a barred gray body. But he was just as dead as any other chicken with a knife wound in the breast.

"The next match will be the last," the referee announced. "After that there'll be the battle royal for all cripples, broken-bills, and stags. This one matches Captain Teach against Spanish Tom."

"That's us, baby!" Uncle Baron said.

Charlie wriggled to the front as Uncle Baron climbed into the pit with the cock. He felt like praying, yet it somehow did not seem right.

Captain Teach bristled up his neck feathers and dropped his head as soon as he saw the big Irish red. On the referee's order, the birds were billed. They struck savagely at each other. Ortiz crooned to his bird in Spanish, while Uncle Baron muttered to his. Then they came back to the scores to wait. The sheaths were drawn.

"Time!"

Charlie whimpered. Both birds flew into the air and started spurring with no preliminary feinting. Feathers flew. The birds fell to earth and circled with heads almost on the ground, neck feathers bristling. Captain Teach seized the other's trimmed comb in his bill and drew blood.

For ten minutes they sparred and flew. "*Cola! Pluma*!" the crowd yelled. Though Charlie saw blood on both birds, he could not tell which was bleeding. It seemed to him that Spanish Tom was a little stronger, because on each fly he rose slightly above the green bird.

At last, both birds were exhausted, and sank to the ground with their heads together.

"Handle!" the referee called.

Uncle Baron breathed on the green bird's comb, nipped it with his teeth. He found a cut on its neck and cauterized the wound with a hot match.

"Pit your birds."

They flew, pecking at each other; they spurred fiercely, and rushed. When the birds lay exhausted once more, the referee called time. Charlie saw, with despair, that Captain Teach was letting the red peck at his eye without turning his head. To his horror, he saw the golden eye go dull and lose a drop of liquid.

"Oh, hell," groaned Uncle Baron.

"Handle," called the referee.

Uncle Baron bared a spot on the green-black tail and blew on it. He nipped the comb vigorously. Then he got a couple of drops of enlivener into the bird's mouth. When the referee called time, he set the bird down with its blind side to the other bird. As soon as he was released, Captain Teach whirled to face the red. They flew up and collided in the air, fell back, and sparred. The red bird flew again. But

Captain Teach was unable to rise. He pecked feebly at Spanish Tom as the red fell on him, gaffs driving at his head. Charlie saw one of the knives go into the dark green neck.

Captain Teach collapsed.

Just like that, it was all over.

Money changed hands. Ed Ortiz counted the bills Uncle Baron handed him. He slapped him on the back. As Uncle Baron leaned over to pick up the dying bird, there came a distant, prolonged honking of a horn.

"*Cops*!" someone shouted.

In seconds, cars were starting and heading off up a back road. Bewildered, Charlie lost track of his uncle in the crowd. When he saw him again, he was at the wheel of the dusty blue bus and it was crowding into the line of fleeing cars. Charlie sprinted and caught up. Running alongside, he tried to open the door. It was locked. He pounded on the door. Uncle Baron looked at him blankly, as though he had never seen him before. Then he called:

"I got to be on the road, Charlie. You see how it is—"

Charlie was puzzled. No: He did not see how it was, except that they had just blown a bundle. But that did not alter their plans.

"Lemme in!" he cried, tugging at the door as the car moved faster.

"Can't, Charlie. Don't you see? Be a good boy, now."

The bus pulled ahead.

Charlie knew he was kidding, but it was a terrible time for jokes. He ran faster, pounding on the window. Uncle Baron set his jaw, gripped the wheel with both hands, and drove on.

"Uncle Baron! I can't—"

The bus was pulling away. He trotted a few yards farther, then stopped and stared. The cars jerked past him. He kept walking, but very slowly now.

After he was sure that his uncle was not coming back and that it was no joke, he stopped walking and leaned against a tree, blind with pain. He did not know he was going to cry until his eyes got hot and the tears spilled out. He turned, pressed his face against the tree, and began to punch it with one fist. His throat ached. He reached up and pressed against his eyes with the thumb and forefinger of one hand, trying to stop the tears, but they kept coming.

Anybody in the world might do a thing like this—anybody but Uncle Baron. Uncle Baron was all fun and gentleness and love. Then why had he done it?

Hearing a car coming, he turned hopefully. But it was a police car. He wiped his eyes and nose on his sleeve, and waited.

Why had he done it?

The squad car halted beside him. In all that recently busy place of men and gamebirds, he was the only living thing left. A policeman in a white helmet, sitting on the passenger's side, stared at him, poker-faced.

"What's going on, son?" he asked sternly.

"Nothing," Charlie said.

"What *was* going on a few minutes ago?"

"Some cockfights," Charlie said.

"Did you know any of the men?" the officer asked.

"No." Charlie blew his nose.

"What's wrong? Are you sick?"

"No."

"And you don't know any of the men who were here?"

"No."

"Let's have it straight, kid."

"It's the truth."

The cop grinned. "Oh, we *know* that! Nobody lies to the *po*lice. We start from that basis and work backward. Come on—get in."

Charlie crawled onto the back seat. There was no inside door handle, and he could not get out now until they let him out. *They can't get me for anything*, he told himself. At least they could not get through the pain in him with any little pains of theirs.

They drove back to thc area called The Hole and

pulled into the parking lot behind a two-story tan brick building: a police station. Then they asked him some more questions. At last the driver spoke into a microphone; then both officers dismounted and one of them let him out of the car.

"Okay," he said. "You can go."

"Where can I get a bus to Ajax Street?" Charlie asked.

"Catch the R bus at the next corner. The driver'll tell you when to transfer."

Chapter 19

The Hundred-Dollar Ladybug

Charlie dragged in at nine o'clock after transferring three times. Clad in a T-shirt, and with no jacket, he was tired and shivering. His pain had turned to numbness. He knew that the numbness, like prehistoric vegetation pressed and pressed until it became coal, would eventually produce the heat called hate.

His father was drinking a can of beer before the television set when he dragged in. Callie was on the telephone, and Buster and his mother were in the kitchen.

"Where's your uncle?" Roscoe Matthews said.

I could come in at 4:00 A.M., Charlie thought, *and he wouldn't give a nickel where I'd been.* He sat on the broken sofa, his legs pulsing with exhaustion.

"I don't know," he said.

"What do you mean, you don't know?"

Charlie's mother and brother drifted in. "Where's Uncle Baron?" Buster asked.

"He split."

"He *split*?" Matthews said. "What's goin' on?"

"Did he tell you about the rooster?" Charlie asked.

Matthews nodded, and laughed. "Lord, the things that man gets into! How'd you make out?"

"It got killed. He bet all our money on it, and we lost it."

"Huh!" Charlie's father said.

"And he drove off and left me when the cops came!" Charlie gazed around at them, wild with anger.

"Well, my land," said his mother. "Ain't that queer?"

"You mean he's *gone*?" Buster asked.

Charlie was close to tears again. "Yes, and I hope he never comes back! He's an old phony! He's a fake!"

"Oh, now, what'd you expect?" said his mother. "Baron is a lot of fun, but he ain't no businessman."

"But I only gave him that money so he'd take me along! And then he dumped me like a dirty shirt."

"Oh, shoot," his father said, turning back to the television set. "What'd you think you was buying, U.S. Steel stock? You shoulda been turning that money over to your family anyhow."

Charlie looked at his mother. She gave him a tired smile. "That's too bad, Charlie," she said. "I got something on the stove." She went back into the kitchen.

Buster came over and sat beside him. "Gee, I'm sorry, Charlie," he said. "How much did you lose?"

"The works."

"What was the cockfight like?"

"Stupid. They fight with little knives on their heels and try to kill each other. The cops hauled me over to the station, but they let me go."

Callie wandered in, having finished her telephone conversation. "What happened? Where's Uncle Baron?"

Charlie got up. "Tell her about it," he mumbled. He punched Buster's shoulder. Buster smiled quickly. He had the right kind of feelings, Charlie decided, even if he didn't know much about life yet.

In bed, he tried to get a good reverie going.

He was riding a big motorcycle down to Caliente where his uncle was working at the racetrack. He wheeled in among the horses Uncle Baron was handling, and they all whinnied and scattered. Charlie roared around for a while, then waved and headed out.

"So long, you old phony!" he called to his uncle.

But it was a feeble daydream, and he let it die.

Through the night, he kept thinking that Uncle Baron would come back. But in the morning the backyard was still deserted.

It was Sunday, a dull day in Dogtown. All day Charlie stewed in boredom and monotony. What surprised him, though it should not have, was that something could happen to you nearly as bad as dying, and no one cared much.

Too bad about you dying, man, they would say.

That was about as close as anybody in this town came to caring.

I'm sorry you had your legs cut off, man, they would say. *Can I have your shoes?*

What a stinking town.

Well, he had the thirty-two dollars left that Uncle Baron must have forgotten about. He had been so excited about buying that bird that he had probably forgotten he had it. It was enough to run away on—but where?

He decided that on Monday he would talk to Leonard and Breathing Man, and at least get a little sympathy. Sympathy would not buy you anything, but it was something he seemed to crave like candy. He was ashamed of needing it, though, and he certainly was not going to ask for it.

When he got up Monday morning, his father was still asleep. Charlie was careful, though, to get out without being caught carrying his schoolbooks. He might work today, or he might go to school. He was glad no one at school knew about Captain Teach. He would have to make up some kind of story.

We bought some pot, and we were going to sell it, but the Nark officers. . . .

But after he reached the shine stand, he did not

want to talk about it even to Leonard. The fire had gone out. To stir it now would only choke him with the cold ash. He had lost something, but he was not sure yet what it was. Leonard asked about Uncle Baron, and Charlie said that he had moved along, that they hadn't gone into that business deal after all. Leonard did not ask him why. He was quiet and gentle.

"You want to do that pair of brown-and-whites?" he asked Charlie. "I think I'll take a little snooze."

It was only eight thirty, early for a snooze; but that was his business. It was not until Leonard had gone in back and closed the door that Charlie understood why he had done it: Mr. Toia's motor was parked at the curb. In his preoccupation with his troubles, he had not heard him coast up. But Leonard had seen him and he was giving them some privacy.

Mr. Toia came toward the shine parlor. His shirt was so bright that it made Charlie blink—yellow and black stripes. Charlie managed to grin when he looked at Mr. Toia, who was smiling at him.

"Well?" the teacher said. That wrapped it all up: *What happened?* he was asking.

All at once Charlie began to choke up. *I am not going to bawl in front of this dude*, he told himself. Because he had just discovered that the fire was not out after all. It was hotter than ever.

"Well, it's a long, sad story," he sighed, shaking

his head. "My uncle and I dissolved the partnership. We split the blanket, man."

"Tell me about it," Mr. Toia suggested.

"We decided it wouldn't work, that's all. He left."

"I guess more things don't work than do," Mr. Toia commented. "It seems to me that's Thing Number One about life. Thing Number Two is that if you keep hammering, something or other usually does."

"Name one thing," Charlie said.

Mr. Toia narrowed his eyes and thought about it. "One thing, for me, is that Charlie Matthews is coming back to school, and next year I'm going to get him a scholarship."

"Who told you that?"

"Just a feeling. How much money did you make?"

"Hundred and eighty-two dollars," Charlie said, surprised at the pride he felt. "In two weeks!"

"You're kidding!" said Mr. Toia, looking surprised.

"No, man."

"Wow! Are you broke now?"

"Not quite."

"A hundred and eighty-two dollars! I don't know a boy, and not many men, who ever made that much money in two weeks. I'm astounded, Charlie. —Did you write it all down?"

"Not yet."

"Put it down, Charlie—put it down! I thought you were going to be a writer. So write! You may feel real sharp about all this right now. But one of these days the edge of it will begin to wear off. And then suppose you want to write a play about it. Where will you get all the details, the sharpness?"

"Okay," Charlie said. "I'll write it tonight."

"By the way—we're starting a new play in class today. Are you going to be there?"

"I'll be over later," Charlie said. "My uncle's gone down to Mexico," he added. "The horses are running at Caliente."

"I see. But you decided not to go along with him?"

Charlie cleared his throat and opened a can of brown polish. "Not exactly. He dumped me."

"Really? Oh, that's too bad." Mr. Toia shook his head. He sat down. "I'm sorry, Charlie. I suppose you know why he did that, don't you?" he asked.

"Because he's a phony," Charlie retorted. "He never did mean to take me with him. It was just a way of getting a stake for a rooster he wanted to buy—a fighting cock. And after he got the money, he blew it. So why stick around?"

Mr. Toia rubbed his jaw. "No, Charlie. He left because he was ashamed. He couldn't face you. If you knew more about him, you'd find that he's been doing things like this all his life—hoping for a strike. The big win, you know? But it never happened. And this time he probably felt worse than he ever felt before, because he'd accidentally tricked his favorite nephew into backing him. Wherever he is, he's got nickels in his pocket and tears in his eyes."

Charlie stood staring at the floor. At last he said: "Maybe you're right. I don't know. I didn't think of it that way."

"I know it's hard to understand," Mr. Toia was saying, "but I'll bet that's it. And in a way, he's done you a favor. He taught you that some people are to love and some are to invest in. And he ran the Dogtown movie fast for you, so that you could see what it's like to be a dropout. All the mean and dirty things you have to do to make a dollar. I don't know all you did to make that money, but it must have been plenty, judging by the bruises on your face."

Very carefully, Charlie applied polish to the shoe he held. Suddenly, from some crevice in his clothing, a ladybug crawled out on his hand. *My last ladybug*, he thought. *All I've got left for my money*. Carefully he plucked it off and dropped it in a drawer. After all, that bug had cost him at least a hundred dollars.

"There's a lot of hard work ahead, Charlie," Mr. Toia was saying. "It's only a year before you'll be scratching for a scholarship. I'll give you all the help I can. I think you can make it. It's just a question of whether you want to make it badly enough."

Walking home after school, Charlie felt better. By some self-vulcanizing process, the leaks in his spirit had begun to heal themselves. Drowsing, he saw himself as the Artful Dodger of Dogtown—smelling out old brick walls to demolish; growing the reddest blood in Dogtown to sell for five dollars a smash; earning a buck here, a buck there, until he made it. He started to fantasy about it, but broke the dream like a stick. It was too much like Uncle Baron's big talk about all the money they were going to make. So, plodding head-down along a sidewalk lined with shaggy old pepper trees, he gave himself over to listing all the bricks walls he could remember in Dogtown, all the mother lodes of old bottles. . . .

In his room that night, he dug out his notebook and lay on his bed chewing the cap of a ballpoint pen. He pondered some titles. *My Uncle Baron: Part Two* And: *How We Caught the Ladybugs.* And: *The Brawl at Legion Hall.* He decided on the ladybug story, and he wrote the title at the top of the page, then printed beneath it, as black as he could:

By Charles B. Matthews